T0064069

The
Guardians
Of Evil

The
Guardians
Of Evil

Baby Kattackal

PARTRIDGE

Print information available on the last page.

To order additional copies of this book, contact
Partridge India
000 800 10062 62
orders.india@partridgepublishing.com

www.partridgepublishing.com/india

Contents

Dedication

To my eldest sister Mrs. Chinnamma Paulose, who inducted me into my literary pursuits.

Preface

A society where scamsters and criminals rule the roost, the rule of law has touched its all-time low. The people are condemned to live a life of insecurity, unable to protest for fear of their dear lives. Virtues have gone down the drain. Its place is usurped by mindless violence. A set of goons thrive, amidst the unwary people, often reared by the politicians to finish their adversaries as part of settling a score with them. And after perpetrating the felony, they remain at large under the protective parasol of the politicians whose *modus operandi* is quite bizarre. They are called 'quotation men' as they quote their fees for killing or chopping the limbs of the people going by the demands of their customers. The worst is that sometimes they kill many hapless innocent people because of mistaken identity. Reckless religious sentiments boost violence, ignoring their noble teachings of universal love. Masquerading of criminals galore as they strategise to protect themselves from being detected. The spread of drugs assumes baffling dimensions with the blessings of the authorities. Those who are supposed to curb their spread feign ignorance of the goings-on in the society. Those who are duty bound to maintain the rule of law show callous indifference to it. They resort to easy ways to shun their duties. A minister's visit is more important for them than a dead body that has surfaced in the river a few minutes ago. Superstitions and blind belief are rampant, which often boomerang, putting the believer in an inescapable bottleneck. A reasonable inquiry into the veracity of such beliefs is absent for fear of the wrath of God. The sanctity and depths of consanguinity is blatantly at stake, causing it to be redefined to suit the present. Our society has turned into a veritable cesspool of all sorts of evils with the inaction of the incumbents . . . And what's surprising is that the responsible incumbents have turned into the protectors of evil . . . Now read on . . . All the best.

Author

Chapter 1

Maxwell paced up and down the patio in front of his house, looking intently at a distant point of the street where the road took a sharp turn to the right. His mind was agitated. He was waiting for someone on a mission, so important to him. So eager to know the outcome of the mission, he whimsically wished the time to pass at a faster pace so that the person would reach him sooner, errand accomplished.

He was in two minds – the one that catered to reality and the other to his fantasy. Both these took active parts in his reverie. His mind of reality reminded him of the old adage: 'time and tide will not wait for any'. Then he thought how stupid he was to think of the time to pass at a faster pace according to his convenience, according to his whims! How silly he was to think of impossibilities, even if it was for a moment! Then he knew it was foolish to think of fantasies to come to reality. But his mind of fantasy that could settle with nothing short of the success of his mission went on telling him "high time the errand brought good tidings of the mission's success . . . It's high time . . . It's high time . . .' Those whimsical whisperings and misty thoughts of his mind of fantasy were quite disturbing to him. He decided to ignore its whimsical urgings and go by the dictates of his mind's realistic part. He repeated, 'Time and tide will not wait for any.'

He thought this notion conveyed the passage of time had a preset speed and its flow was perennial according to nature's set pattern which could never be changed according to human whims and fancies It could never be limited or otherwise tampered by human agency according to man's wish or desire. This was what was exactly meant by the aphorism. This led him to coin a new theory: 'unlimited time, illimitable by human fantasy'. Each moment he was getting more and more realistic. The reason for his initial whimsical thought was because his self-set time limit, within which he had expected the person to come back, mission completed, was soon to be over. Now he realized the wait could be longer than expected. A new finding cropped up in his mind – the uselessness of being in a hurry. He realized it wasn't the time but more importantly the success of the mission that counted. He was brought face-to-face with truth. This knowledge obliterated from his mind his self-set whimsical constraints of time within which he expected the mission to be complete. As the rigours of the time limit set by him faded away, he relaxed. Then his attention turned to the passers-by on the road. They were of assorted types, no doubt. Some were agile and fast while some were clumsy and slow. But he knew they all had a purpose – to meet their day's needs whatever they may be that had brought them out of the confines of their homes. But their speed or slowness was never an indication of the urgency of their mission. It was their natural deportment that made the difference. No one could get over the inherent delay in a task to be completed as so many rigid factors beyond human comprehension and calculations were involved in the process. He knew this was a universal truth. And it was this thought that took away the urging factor from his mind. He turned, mellowed. He turned more and more realistic. The initial lopsided stubborn view of his uncompromising mind that wanted his mission to be a success at any cost, within the time stipulated, was replaced with his new-found sagacity, wisdom, and a strange kind of give-and-take view of compromise.

This state of his mind unravelled before him a new philosophy of life. He knew the success of his mission would bring him happiness and hopes. But if his mission failed . . . ? He could find this question realistic in more ways than one, though he couldn't find an instant answer to it. But he knew the normal answer was frustration. His changed mental condition of sagacity, wisdom, etc. never allowed him to drown in frustration and give up for good. Then he hit upon a practical and realistic philosophy based on equanimity – to view life's setbacks and achievements with more poise and composure. He believed only frustrations gave rise to hopes. Human life was a strange blend of so many frustrations and hopes, for each frustration engendered new hope. This may sound strange, but to Maxwell it was so. The absence of frustration made his hopes lustreless and infructuous. Such a condition brought him hopelessness and frustrations. To him, he was a lone traveller along a narrow pathway in a countryside bordered with tall trees and undergrowth. Suddenly, the sun brightened up. And the trees traced dark patterns on the pathway. Now the pathway was neither with shadows alone nor with sunlight alone. They were interlaced. They were a combination of the opposites. Strangely, they were complementary, not competitive as was the wont when opposites met. Beyond the shadow, there were bright patches of sunlight. To him, the shadows represented human frustrations and the bright patches of sunlight beyond represented hopes in human life. So it was frustration that gave rise to hopes according to him. 'Beyond every shadow there was bright sunlight. Beyond every frustration there was hope.' It was his philosophy. Dissecting human life around, his finding was that life was an admixture of opposites – governed by the unquestioned law of the harmony of the opposites.

Night began to fall. A pervasive darkness made the visibility poor. People on the road were still passing him from both directions. As they moved away from him, they assumed ghostly figures and finally disappeared from view. Maxwell still kept on waiting. The wait lasted an hour before he spotted a spectral figure, negotiating the distant curve on the road and moving towards his direction. In the poor visibility, he felt this spectral figure too assumed so many spooky shapes, and as it came closer and closer, the increase in proximity gave it the hazy shape of a human. Amidst the dreariness of a long wait, he experienced the first stirrings of new hopes . . .

Chapter 2

Vypeen, surrounded by the backwaters of Vembanadu, was an island of splendour. The waves from the backwaters incessantly washed the shores wet, which glistened under the sun. The wet glow gave the shore a molten look, as though the shore was melting into the waters under the scorching sun. The surging waves frothed against the shore one after another, as if adorning it with silver anklets. This was the essence of the island's natural charm which age or passage of time could never blot out or mar. The abundant coconut groves – the wealth of the island – gave its foliage alluring, uniform look. Their fronds gleefully swayed and danced nonstop, fuelled by the incessant gusts of winds from the backwaters. This ambience provided an appropriate backdrop for the vibrant life of the Vypeenites – full of drama.

The labour class consisted of fishermen, coconut-pluckers, and toddy tappers as well as those who worked in taverns, toddy parlours, and government licensed distilleries. They outnumbered the rich. This was the place where poverty and profligacy met with good grace. Harmony existed between the poor and the rich. This was the haven of *Abkaris*, the government licensees who sold toddy and arrack and earned a fortune. No wonder, toddy parlours were pitched everywhere. The *Abkaris* always believed they had created a life for these labourers. But to the labourers, life was what was happening to them, in their day-to-day existence. They never looked forward to their uncertain future. They were concerned only with the immediate present. To them, life was to be enjoyed to the maximum at low cost. This attitude of the labour class well catered to the perennial inflow of pungent, spurious, cheap liquors called hooch. The labourers after a hard day's toil and moil wanted leisure which did not mean rest, but relaxation to them. They wanted all their nerves, which had swathed their muscles tight and stiff because of the day's hard labour, to unwind. This was what was meant by relaxation for them. When the nerves started to unwind, it was a kind of floating sensation they were in. Then they forgot all their woes and miseries of life. They felt they were exalted to a higher mental level, and that was what they wanted themselves to be in. They staggered around gleefully, their feet barely touching the ground, and indistinctly prattled inanities with a heavy tongue. But the sprightly story of the island life was marred by the shadow of an occasional hooch tragedy and other mishaps.

The islanders, never considered hooch death a tragedy. But only to the people outside the island. When they drink poisonous hooch, they all know the possibility of death. But unmindful, they drink it in a good measure to be high. Before the sheen of life's enjoyment, death is only a damp squib to them. It's part of the stride in the sense if birth is the beginning of life, death is its inevitable end, whenever and whatever manner it happens. But whatever be the cause, death is able to kill a man only once in his lifetime. This aphorism, in the same measure, is applicable to those who consume hooch and those who don't. Not all who consume hooch are victims of hooch tragedy or have an early death. But such a mishap happens spontaneously and once in a while. Avoiding hooch for fear of death, which is a one-time event in human life, is like forsaking the so many occasions of pleasures provided by hooch. It's foolish to say death in any form and at any time is a tragedy just because it puts an end to human life. This is so because death is not a separate entity that visits a random few only, sparing others, but an integral part of the life of the entire humanity. Any person born into this world would die one day and he has to accept it as part of the stride, that it's part of human life, that it's inevitable, that it's the end of a beginning, sometime ago. Even a man of so many achievements in life is not spared of death. But can his life be called a tragedy when death puts an end to it? Or for that matter, can his death be called a tragedy? The uncertainty of death makes the pleasures of life significant for making use of the opportunity fully before death visits a person. This is the islanders' philosophy of life. But they never knew it had an ancient parallel which had its origin long ago. They never knew Omar Khayyam. Never read his *Rubaiyat*. Never heard of the Epicurean philosophy or never heard of those famous lines, which precisely conveyed his philosophy of life: 'Eat, drink and enjoy', when he blithesomely crooned:

And with a loaf of bread beneath the bough,
A book of verses, a flask of wine,
And thou singing beside me, in the wilderness"
Oh! the wilderness is paradise enow.

But nevertheless, the islanders unwittingly put to practice the pleasure-seeking philosophy of eat, drink, and enjoy as if it was originally coined by them, not even having an inkling that it had an ancient parallel. And the labour class lived on, unmindful of the mishaps in their lives.

It was long since the last hooch deaths had taken place. Then there was a respite. The incident seemed to have been a thing of the past and very well forgotten by the islanders. Thus, the island life passed uneventfully for some time. Then something happened. Something so serious.

Chapter 3

The house in Vypeen, overlooking the backwaters of Vembanadu, was dilapidated and rickety. It was unkempt with creepers straggling on its lime-plastered walls and roof. The walls were mildewed and dotted with cracks and blisters from where earthen, saffron, thin snake-like termitaries emerged as if snakes slithering out of their burrows. The tiny roots of the creepers found their easy way through the cracks to have a vice-like grip on the laterite stones beneath, which prevented them from falling down in a heap in the incessant winds from the backwaters. The edges of the doors, windows, and door frames of the house were blunted, moth-eaten. The kitchen was all too small and smoke-begrimed. Rodrigues, 50, the father of the house, short and plump with a rotund face; a security personnel in the nearby Zenith Distillery, lived here with two more souls – his wife Mildred, forty-five years old, a tall and beautiful but glum-faced lady, destined to suffer subjugation at the hands of her drunkard husband, and their son, Maxwell, twenty-three years old, tall and handsome with light blue eyes, the spitting image of his mother. Studying in the final year of Bachelor of Education course, he was a hapless dependent on his father, destined to suffer in silence the goings-on in the house. The mother and the son lived on, with painful thoughts and disquieting expectation of a quarrel when the drunkard father was home every night, fully lit up. The family had a hand-to-mouth existence on the pittance brought home by the father after lavishing on liquors which was his first passion. The income was insufficient for the family and more importantly for the education of Maxwell.

Chapter 4

One day, there was an unseasonable cloudburst. It was raining cats and dogs with heavy winds. Then suddenly the thought of the havoc created by the previous years' monsoon in which so many coconut trees were uprooted and so many fishermen had lost their lives in the cyclonic winds flashed in the mind of Mildred. She remembered how the fallen coconuts floating in the backwaters were cradled by the waves that rose ferociously in the winds. At that time, so many fishing canoes and a boat were drowned. Two days after, the debris along with some corpses were found stranded on a desolate shore while some were still floating around, in the backwaters, pushed and pulled by the waves.

Mildred was apprehensive of how far the house could withstand the ensuing monsoon going by the atrocities created by the previous year's monsoon. She made a mental calculation and found out only three more months were left for the next monsoon to reach Vypeen. She felt she was a bit late in addressing the problem. Though Maxwell, her son, was more obsessed with the shabby looks of the house, she brought her apprehensions to his notice as an intense, potential danger, before presenting it before her temperamental husband. But Maxwell showed the least interest in it, saying casually, 'You're already late. But that's no matter. I tell you it's better late than never.' Notwithstanding her son's casual attitude, she decided to present the problem to her husband. But she had to wait for the right opportunity.

The public too were bothered about the outward shabby looks of the house. And it was the looks that invited derisive comments from them. Mildred thought the public's comments had some substance too, though she was more concerned with the stability of the house. But Maxwell and Mildred had to put up with it, while Rodrigues alone was unmindful and nonchalant.

Those ignorant locals who were crude and manner-less had a penchant for interfering with other's affairs and they used to pass derisive comments about the condition of the house. Some thought Rodrigues was the victim of some strange spell and perverted visions. If any of such comments reached Rodrigues's ears, he would pick on the particular person and groan, 'It seems you are beastly suburban. You have a discomforting, irresistible itch to mock at my house. In fairness, I tell you, you're free to give it a new look, of course, at your own expense, and if you could relieve yourself from such discomforts that way, I shall be happy. Or else you better mind your own business and that will stand you in good stead.' Those who chanced to get the deriding retort from Rodrigues felt as if they had got a sudden punch on their faces for poking their noses unnecessarily into others' affairs. (Such comments would normally go unnoticed or discarded or not taken seriously. But Rodrigues wasn't one such.) It taught the ignorant villagers of Vypeen a lesson in manners, which was not known to them before, that it was not fair to interfere in others' affairs unnecessarily.

Maxwell didn't agree with his father's attitude towards such people, when he came to know of it. He knew his father was wrong. It was his father's fault that invited public comments. He thought his father's response to it was a kind of escapism, a cover for his irresponsible ways. He told this to his mother.

'What's there if people comment when there is truth? One cannot always castigate such comments as unnecessary interference in others affairs. Father may be able to silence the people, but he will not be able to convince them by cogent reasoning,' Maxwell spoke in a low voice, as he wanted only his mother to hear his opinion.

'The maintenance work on our house is overdue. But it's never the business of others to pass comments. Even if Father failed in his duty, it's none of their concern. If anything, we're the people to be bothered.' Mildred supported her husband, though in the deep recess of her heart, she didn't agree with his omissions.

'What angered Father is his wounded prestige and not any offensive act on the part of the public towards him. Everyone expects or wants to command a kind of pre-eminence in the society in which he lives,' Maxwell spoke in a philosophical vein.

'Well, what you mean by the word "pre-eminence"?' Mildred asked inquisitively. She couldn't grasp the meaning.

'Mom, it's one's desire to be respected by others in the society. Do you get me?' Maxwell explained, still doubtful if his explanation had made things clear to her.

'Yes, Son. But can't someone also command respect from people by himself adopting a policy of non-interference in other's affairs?' Mildred asked as clarification. Mildred was not one to jump into conclusions. Long years of servitude under Rodrigues had taught her patience. Sometimes, it gave her a penchant to support her husband by submitting meekly to his views when others tried to find fault him. And it was this attitude that made her ask such questions.

'No. One cannot command respect from others by his adopting a policy of non-interference in others' affairs. What I feel is, in such cases, one has a duty to others too by adopting for himself a socially acceptable way of life, which is not incumbent on one to be so, though,' Maxwell replied.

'But what in your father's case is his socially acceptable duty to others? You mean your father has something more to do, something more impressive, to be in a position of pre-eminence, to keep his prestige intact?' Mildred pushed her son a step forward towards the point she wanted to know so that she could get an answer from her son's mouth itself rather than going in for her own conclusions.

'He should establish a reputation by his good conduct, which is very significant. People would assess if his conduct is acceptable and appreciable to the society and pass their opinions, which is not any kind of interference on their part but their right as part of their living in a society. Assessing a person by others is not just interfering with that person's affairs. And if Father's actions are in conformity with the expectations of the people, then the respectability automatically comes his way.' Maxwell's calm temper, whenever he spoke to his mother, made him explain things to her in a soft way, which brought to her mind something like enlightenment.

'What you said is right. Your father's conduct has never been a respectable one. He drinks and indulges in drunken brawls. Everyone knows that.' Mildred added to her son's views as if she was convinced, though initially she took exceptions.

'The maintenance work of the house, though long overdue, is not the thing that invites derisive comments from the people around. It's the shabby looks and the aberrant nature of Father. Who could ever keep his house covered with wild creepers in abundance and fondly nurse the saffron snake-like termitaries on the walls? This peculiar look of our house could never escape public attention. Actually, Father is playing it into the hands of the public and inviting their adverse comments unwittingly. Father has to admit that people in a society are like that. So there's no point in his finding fault with them. What I feel is, if anything, it's nothing but his own failure and irresponsible ways of living that invite people's adverse comments. And for that he is not to find fault with the public. But he has to look within himself and mend his ways,' Maxwell said.

Her son's talk in detail made Mildred happy. She could detect a glint of his confidence and sagacity in it. She felt the way her son analysed the whole matter was superb.

'Son, you're a good teacher in the making. You have selected the right course for you. You will shine in it. Your patient interpretation of the situation with such incisive clarity and logic made a convincing effect on me. Now I understand Father's view that people are interfering with his own private affairs is just to cover his own faults, which has no justification. He has no convincing reasoning for his own omissions. This situation puts him in a blind alley. Now I realise it's an effective bulwark for him to silence others. People adopt this tactics as a last resort to beat their opponents, when they know they themselves are at fault,' Mildred said, unusually happy.

To Maxwell, his mother's expression was new. She was always sad and agitated in her life, always being in anxious expectation of something that put her in difficulties. It made her mind depressed and agitated.

'Mom, now you have a new look. What makes you unusually happy?' Maxwell asked.

'Don't you know what makes me happy? It's my realization that you're not subdued by your father's heartless, unconcerned talk about you. Normally, anybody would be affected by such an ambience at home. But you have a rigid personality that will not get affected by any such circumstance in life. Besides, I'm sure you're capable of outliving any adverse situation in your life with considerable aplomb. I realize you're sensible. You're capable of a deep study of your father's aberrant nature with utmost shrewdness. It makes my duty easy. Now it's confined to the work of teaching you a little bit of patience to put up with Father. Now I'm happy, yes, perhaps the happiest.' Mildred's eyes were moist with joy when she said this.

Maxwell saw in her eyes a deep affection for him. He saw in her eyes the endless love of a mother for her son, which gave him added confidence and enthusiasm. When he analysed his father's response to public criticism, he felt his father was a failure with the public also. When he told about his findings to his mother, she had no qualms in changing her view and joining those of her son's. Maxwell thought his mother was not carried away totally by her life of servitude under Father. Sagacity and wisdom were still in her, behind her life of servitude.

Chapter 5

One day, a favourable opportunity came Mildred's way. It was a Sunday. Rodrigues's friends King and Roger came visiting him. Among friends, he was always a changed man – in a good mood, chatting and cracking jokes. Mildred took this as the best time for her to present the problem to him.

She came out of the kitchen and stood behind him. Roger and King were sitting opposite, facing her. They knew she was up to something. She hemmed and hawed to attract the attention of Rodrigues. But it was not of any use. Rodrigues was feigning that he had not noticed her presence behind him. After some time, she withdrew into the kitchen. Rodrigues's talk with friends continued. Mildred again came out of the kitchen. This time she positioned herself at a point from where she and Rodrigues could see each other.

'I'm here to present to you an important problem,' Mildred introduced the subject.

'I know. Whenever you come to me, there is a problem,' Rodrigues said.

'But this is a serious one,' Mildred said.

'Every problem is serious. That's why we call it a problem,' Rodrigues said.

Mildred knew Rodrigues would not give due importance to what she had to say.

But still she ventured to present it.

'Our house is in a dilapidated condition as we all know. It would not stand the next monsoon unless something is done to make it strong. I need not remind you of the havoc created by the last monsoon' Mildred said.

'It seems you have a special knack to come to the wrong decision whenever a right decision is expected of you,' Rodrigues said derisively.

'I'm not taking any decision. I'm only presenting to you a probable situation and its unhappy consequences,' Mildred said.

'I tell you, don't be over-anxious about it. It would tell upon your health. Why invite trouble? It has the strength to withstand any weather. That's why it could survive all the previous monsoons,' Rodrigues replied.

'If you ignore it, you would have to spend more than what you have to spend now. Remember, a stitch in time saves nine,' Mildred said.

'I would as well tell you an untimely stitch is a waste too. Then you don't have to worry too much about it. I will tackle any problem as and when it comes. That's my policy. There is no point in anticipating a problem and spending a fortune on it. Whenever you approach me with a problem, it would invariably cause a drain on my pocket. And now I would suggest a way for you to tackle the problem in which no money is involved. But I very much need your cooperation. Are you game for it?' Rodrigues asked.

The big idea of solving the problem without spending any money made Mildred happy. She became more enthusiastic. 'If you need my cooperation, why you doubt? I'm very much here to help you. Is it not the duty of a dutiful wife to help her husband in whatever way, when he is in need of her help?

I hope you remember I have been a dutiful wife to you and you can be sure I would be the same wife to you in future also. And let us jointly take preventive measures to keep our house intact. So tell me! I'm anxious to hear from your mouth what help I could give you. And take it from me, whatever help you need, it would be done without as much as a murmur on my part. You can believe me 100 per cent,' Mildred said happily.

A smile writ large on Rodrigues's face, which no one noticed. Then he said, 'I need your cooperation in your not troubling me with this problem any more.' Rodrigues had a hearty laugh. He looked at his friends, expecting they too would be laughing at his rejoinder. But they weren't.

Rodrigues after dismissing Mildred's requests summarily was happy he could outlive the situation without disclosing his reasons for keeping the house in its present condition. His attitude prompted Maxwell to find out his father's secret reasons for rejecting Mildred's request. So he decided not to give up his attempt. He resorted to many plausible ways to find out. But the more Maxwell was adamant in knowing the reason, the more Mildred became anxious and agitated for obvious reasons. Mildred's attitude worried him. But his inquisitiveness got the better of him every moment. He was obsessed with the question as to why his father was silent about the shabby looks of the house inviting public derision and what made him so adamant to abstain from doing something to have the problem licked.

'He's a silly bum, a monster who never speaks sense,' Mildred thought, frustrated, after hearing Rodrigues's evasive answer to her request.

But her thought was momentary, impulsive, out of a sudden spurt of disgust, which made her different from her usual self.

She was soon back to her natural self, thinking that she shouldn't have thought of her husband that way.

Mildred was sad. Though she had learnt over the years to put up with her husband's irresponsible ways and silly talk, she wondered how she had a momentary change of mind to think about her husband that way, which was unlikely of her.

Maxwell was very much there to answer her question. 'Mom, your thoughts about Father were nothing but the sudden outburst of a natural yet suppressed human feeling. But why your mind attaches so much importance to it? Keeping yourself worried over something silly is your own fault. If your such thoughts about father were something bad, they don't make you an entirely bad woman. And for that matter every human being is at once good and bad,' Maxwell philosophized.

'How come?' Mildred asked inquisitively, coming out of her dejected mood. She had a sudden feeling that her son's philosophy was quite intriguing.

'He's good when his cultivated habits of sagacity, wisdom, care, compassion, and tolerance that are part of his civilised mind govern him and bad when he is at times governed by his inborn, instinctive mind, I mean his uncivilised, primitive, selfish mind,' Maxwell said.

'You said something to mean human virtues are cultivated. Now what makes you think so?' Mildred cut in.

'I tell you. The so-called virtues are man's acquired ones. God made man with a primitive mind with animal instincts sans virtues and gave a code of virtues in the form of the Ten Commandments for him to follow. This is why I used the word "cultivated" to mean the virtues weren't inborn but acquired ones,' Maxwell said.

'Then what happened to his primitive characteristic?' Mildred asked as if she was hearing a new story.

'Man did not change *in toto*. His primitive mind with its savage characteristics was his genuine mind over which a superstructure of a mind of virtues came into being, on his acquiring culture and civilisation,' said Maxwell.

'But didn't God preach virtues to man through his Ten Commandments?' Mildred asked.

'Yes, the Ten Commandments preached virtues, and slowly, man acquired culture and civilisation. But then his acquired virtues couldn't hold on long against the pressure of his primitive mind's instinctive feelings. This situation was something called 'man against himself'. A slow but steady tussle between his instinctive savage mind and his mind of virtues was going on in him ever since, in which we see his mind of virtues turning the underdog. This process is slow and we could see the slow erosion of virtues from our society,' Maxwell said.

'So you mean the Ten Commandments have lost its relevance in the modern world causing the exit of virtues? And then whose is the fault for this sorry state of affairs?' Mildred asked.

'Mom, your question is a genuine and significant one. But before answering it, let me ask you quite a few questions. Have you ever put a thought to the question why God created man with a primitive mind initially when he could have installed a virtuous mind in its place that generated only virtuous thoughts in him? Then God would have been fair in his dealings with his chosen creation called man. Then he could have been quite at peace with humanity. And why did he wait till his creation works were over to give him some guidelines to be virtuous in the form of the Ten Commandments? I ask these questions because the believers say nothing is impossible with God. But I feel God failed here, blundered or bungled,' Maxwell replied.

'It's perhaps God wanted his creation to taste the satanic evils and godly virtues to make his own choice to follow,' Mildred said.

'So God knowingly gave his creations an opportunity to taste both evil and virtues, according to you?' Maxwell asked.

'Yes, that's my belief,' Mildred replied.
'Why must he?' Maxwell asked.

'Perhaps he wanted to test man how deep is his belief in God, given a choice to opt between good and bad,' Mildred replied.

'But it's believed God is omniscient. Then what's the need for him to test man to find out when he could very well anticipate things? God, the all-knowing, should have saved man by creating him with a virtuous mind rather than leaving him high and dry with a primitive mind. And no wonder man couldn't resist for long his temptation to go by his instinctive evil ways,' Maxwell said.

'Then can't man be virtuous even within his primitive mind when the Ten Commandments are there to guide him?' Mildred asked.

'No. The irresistible evil tendencies of man are more powerful than the virtues preached by the Ten Commandments. They are subjective, natural, and instinctive.

But virtuosity is acquired. It's objective in the sense that others are benifited as it calls for sacrifice for others. Who is bothered about the welfare of others. Everyone is in a rat-race for self aggrandizement at any cost. And this is the reason for the proliferation of evil in human society. And what I feel is: Now God must be regretting his big blunder of creating man with a primitive mind, seeing his teachings of virtues are blatantly violated by him,' Maxwell said.

He continued . . .

'So the reason for the evil to stay in the society rests in man himself, glorified as the noble creation of God. One has only to look within to find out. We all join hands surreptitiously to defeat our noble, virtuous mission of driving the evil away from the society. People of all walks of life – sneaky, amorous, religious men out teaching morals; crafty political men who vow in public for the integrity, morality, and sacrifice for the welfare of the society; foxy policemen – dancing to the distorted tunes of the politicians for benefits. None is the better. Everyone is a whitewashed sepulchre with nauseating stink of evil inside,' Maxwell said.

Then he told his mother about her momentary flash of disgust and contrition at something so insignificant to be ignored, which didn't deserve to be subjected even to a momentary thought.

Mildred listened to Maxwell in rapt attention. She felt she couldn't succeed in convincing him about her own views of God and his creations. She found her own arguments were based on belief, pure and simple. She was sure she wouldn't be able to cut her son's logic. So she opted to reply in a vague manner to close the topic.

'Son, yours are cogent views based on logic. But mine is based on belief. And no believer would ever agree with your views. Logic is always good. Logical questions are cogent. But sometimes cogency is for cogency's sake only. Your cogent questions sometimes look wise, but truth may be otherwise,' Mildred replied.

Mildred's vague reply put an end to their talk. And this made her gloat secretly at her success in being vague. But she never had any inkling that her son had an impious face. She realised that her son was blasphemous, which made her sad. But she knew she couldn't convince him of God and his virtuous ways. She knew she wasn't well armed to confront him with her views of God. So she kept quiet for the better, leaving the topic . . .

Chapter 6

Maxwell and Mildred were afraid of cleaning the walls off the termitaries and trimming the creepers, fearing they would be inviting trouble from Father. It looked as if the father found some strange pleasure in keeping his wife and son in the dark about his strange ways. His attitude was such as if his wife and son didn't matter much to him for discussing such matters with them. The mother and the son thought the father's ways were inconceivable and bizarre, crossing the limits of reasonableness. But none of them could find out the reason. So the only way available to them was to do some guesswork based on conjectures.

Maxwell initially thought of it as one of the eccentricities of his father, the roots of which were unknown to him. Mildred thought of the reason as Rodrigues's indifference in keeping the building strong and neat despite her so many requests. Another reason ascribed to Rodrigues's act was his miserliness in spending money on repair works. Maxwell had yet another reason to believe that drunkards were generally shabby and his reluctance to do the repair works was a fallout of that habit. All these were their initial guesswork. So many similar inferences passed through their minds that was boggled over the issue. It was as if Mildred and Maxwell were thrown into a veritable swirl of guesswork; their so many reasons twirled like swirling mists in their minds. Then a philosophical notion dawned on Maxwell – none could successfully make a guesswork about the real reasons behind the act of another. A seemingly plausible way to find out was to make that particular act of another (which is the external manifestation of his thoughts) available for a thorough scrutiny by the person making the guess.

This makes the guess more complex, and hence chances are very much there for the assessment to go wrong. This is because the reasons guessed by the person (purporting to be the real one) behind the act of another are vitiated by his own subjectivity. So the reasons from guesswork need not be real. Each man is trapped in his own subjective pattern or subjectivity and so is his thinking process. Here the interplay of the subjective factors of both the persons makes the chances of arriving at a correct finding bleak. A man's subjectivity sets the pattern of his own thinking process which would be different from that of another in an identical situation. This is why two people have different findings about the same act or incident or whatever it is when they are put to guesswork. The person making the assessment believes or can only believe his assessment is nothing but true. This is because he can't think beyond his pattern. A different thought can never occur to him except according to his own pattern or subjectivity. It was such a situation that Mildred and Maxwell were in.

Realising that there was substance in such thoughts, Maxwell was the first to come out of the swirl. It was a real escape for him. With great relief, he thought, 'It's better not to waste time indulging in guesswork.'

Then he declared in a generalized manner, 'Mom, it could be one of the so many perversions of Father.'

'Perversion? I can't even guess any. But I feel he is of quirky habits,' Mildred said, confused, torn between the two words, not knowing the exact difference in their connotations.

'But there must be something even behind a man's quirky actions. It could be a silly one. But anyway, he owes us an explanation. But he isn't likely to come out with his own explanation. So I think I must ask him,' Maxwell asserted, no more interested in guesswork. He wanted to salvage his mother too from the swirl of guesswork.

Maxwell's statement of 'I think I must ask him' was not acceptable to Mildred. The possible confrontation between the father and the son roused disquieting thoughts in her.

'But you're not going to get a reply from him. Don't you know his nature? Then, my son, why do you speak as if you're unaware of it? You should remember he hasn't opened his mind to us so far. What does it mean? It's because he wants it to be kept as a secret. Or if at all you could get a reply from him, it would be a white lie. So what is the purpose of just asking him when you're sure to get a wrong answer and get yourself knowingly fooled?' Mildred said, with a discouraging and disquieting expression on her face. She actually wanted to avoid a father–son confrontation. She was always in anxious expectation of something momentous and undesirable happenings whenever the son chanced to face the father. And she earnestly believed it was her duty to prevent such a situation at any cost.

'It's for the sake of my son's future,' she thought on such occasions.

'Your reasoning may be correct. But you have to realise he is of impudent nature, and if he doesn't want to reveal, you're likely to get a reply: "It's none of your business". That sounds like: who are you to question me? Then you would get hurt. Why make such a nasty situation? You aren't going to gain anything, if at all his reasons are made known to you. And you aren't going to lose anything if his reasons aren't made known to you. He won't change his ways,' Mildred said softly with an air of firmness. But in her heart she was suppressing her distress and anxiety. She felt she could never go wrong in her assessments of her husband; that's what her own long experience as his wife had taught her. And it was this thought that caused distress and anxiety in her mind. She knew the probable eventuality of a talk between the father and the son would end up in an angry showdown. She was anxious about the situation going out of hand.

'But whatever be, it cannot be left out in this manner. It's our right to know. It's a question of our family's prestige. Don't you think so?' Maxwell quite rightly reasoned.

'What is the point in just knowing the reasons if you can't change him at all? I tell you one thing. You aren't to rack your brain. You would do well to divert your thoughts to something more important . . .,' Mildred stopped halfway through. She seemed to have been prevented from completing the sentence as if something had interrupted her thoughts.

But Maxwell seemed to be more concerned with the question why his father was so concerned about keeping the termitaries and the creepers intact. The thought in his mind became such an obsession that he couldn't attach importance to anything else. But suddenly something flashed in his mind. It was the thought of giving a patient hearing to his dear mother, which brought him back to what his mother was about to tell him.

'Mom, why did you stop halfway? Tell me what are you up to? Is it something you don't want to tell me?' Maxwell asked, confused.

'Nothing of that sort, Son. But I think the integrity of our family is more important than prestige,' Mildred expressed her opinion. She was sure her son would never agree with her. That was the thought that made her diffident initially – to tell or not to tell.

'To me, it appears prestige is more important than the integrity of the family,' Maxwell replied softly. But he seemed to stick to his view sternly, all the same.

Suddenly she thought his answer showed the naivety and inexperience of a youth who has only just crossed his teens.

'You speak like an immature youth. It's your youthful vanity and ardour that make you say so. You think you're knowledgeable, which you're not so much as you think of yourself. You haven't had enough time to gain maturity through experience. You seem to forget it was not long before you were in my arms. It was not long before you were off my teats. You have yet to go a long way to mature,' Mildred said.

'I think it's prestige that brings a kind of pre-eminence to our family. It makes us respectable before the public. Respectability creates high esteem among the people with which they view us. Then we will be known to all and sundry as persons who belong to a family of high repute, as persons who keep its prestige high and intact. And shouldn't this aspect be more significant to us than integrity? I don't understand what makes you think differently,' Maxwell spoke again in a mild way. He didn't want to turn the talk into an argument, which would hurt his mother. It was his sensitive thoughts for his mother's sufferings because of an unkind man of quirky habits, not at all deserving to be called her husband, which made him all love and kindness for her.

There was an uncanny rapport between the mother and the son. The mother was quite sympathetic towards the son as she knew her husband didn't have a concern for his only son, which should have been born out of a genuine love for him. Maxwell had utmost concern and sympathy for his mother as he felt she was a scapegoat, destined always to be at the receiving end of his father's blows. There were occasions when the mother and the son held different views. But the difference was strangely enveloped in a kind of rapport between them, even when they disagreed. It looked as if the mother and son agreed even when they disagreed.

'My mother is a sacrificial goat. She isn't the wife of my father but a slave of him, condemned to live like that all her life. She can't rise to the level of a free woman with a free will, because hers is always a subdued soul,' Maxwell thought of her sympathetically. Then a strange kind of aversion came to the fore in his mind towards his father.

'Mom, you're extremely soft. Women shouldn't be like that. I see you always in a submissive mood. Your life with your husband who bullies you, who speaks to you with his sinewy arms, makes you submissive. I don't know if you ever had a mind to have a fighting spirit against the odds in your life. Yours is a kind of mere existence, which is as good as you're non-existent in this world,' Maxwell said.

'Do you mean mine is a purposeless existence? Your words seem to mean so,' Mildred asked a little bit sadly.

'You don't have any initiative, I think. My father's strong-armed ways made you so.' Maxwell softly opened up his heart about his mother, though he was guided with a kind of warm concern for her.

'But, Son, I'm purposeful. I have a goal in life. But my ways are soft and amicable, keeping in tune with the ambience in our family. It's not lack of any initiative on my part. It isn't any lack of purpose. I'm strong in my goal. My silence and amicable ways only show my ardour to achieve my goal, waging a silent war against the odds in my life, I'm put to fight with. I have never lost sight of my goal. I never can. If I'm to lose sight of my goal, it's as good as I forget you, which I tell you can never be. You don't know what's going on in me. It's a struggle to achieve my goal. You don't know how I fight the odds in my life to live on till I achieve my goal. You can't see the intensity of my persistence and perseverance to achieve it. You don't know how unrelenting I'm, how stern and stubborn I'm. You don't know how much I'm preoccupied with my goal. But you see only my silence and silence alone, and you can take it only as my timidity.' Mildred's voice was soft, but her eyes reflected her calm resolve.

'My son has to be trained in patience for his own sake, for his own well-being in future. He has to be equipped to face life valiantly with a kind of calm sagacity – an academic degree for which he has to be submissive to his father to a great extent. He has to keep him in good humour. And it's my bounden duty to guide him, to teach him patience, to teach him how to be submissive, how not to hurt his volatile father, till he passes out, for which I have to be vigilant. I have to be keen on avoiding the father–son confrontations. It calls for my efficient involvement to avoid situations or settle problems in an amicable manner,' Mildred soliloquised. Then she came back to the question they were discussing.

'Son, the prestige of our family cannot be kept intact however keen we are and whatever precautions we take,' Mildred replied.

'What makes you think so?' Maxwell sought a clarification from his mother.

'I mean, you and I alone cannot keep the prestige of our family. Whatever effort we put to keep it through our good conduct, your father's wayward ways of life cause it to go down the drain. It's as if we cannot contain him. Then how can we keep up the prestige of our family? Any aberrant member of a family can destroy its prestige,' Mildred said sadly. She looked forlorn.

'You mean Father too should be cooperative when it comes to keeping our family's prestige up?' Maxwell asked.

'Yes, Son. It goes without saying. Your father's acts are not at all in conformity with the prestige of our family. He is a drunkard. He indulges in street brawls. He never cares to keep our house neat and tidy. He never allows to wipe off the termitaries. He never allows anyone to cut and remove the overgrown creepers over the house. He is guided by some sort of quirky obsessions. That's what I feel. Such people believe by keeping things intact in a particular way fortune would come to them. Our house now looks like a house fallen into disuse, its inhabitants having long abandoned it. Nobody would believe that three souls exist in it even now,' Mildred said.

Then a sudden nostalgia overwhelmed her and she was sad. A conflict arose in her mind about a family life of her expectation and the present one in which she was. It caused her eyes to smart. Maxwell noticed it and he thought his mother was agitated.

'But wouldn't father's wayward ways affect the integrity of our family as well?' Maxwell raised yet another doubt. The question had two purposes. Firstly, he noticed his mother's eyes were moist, which showed she was emotional and he wanted to bring her back from that mood. Secondly, he wanted a clarification from his mother for his question.

'When it comes to the integrity of our family, we can keep it intact by our own contributions. The antagonistic behaviour of a member of the family need not cause its disintegration, if the other members of the family are ready to bear with the odd one. Others can keep up its integrity through their sacrifice in this way. Then integrity is more to life than prestige. So the term is more meaningful to family life. It's not just a case of touch and go as in the case of the family's prestige. And take it from me, prestige is a mushroom with no roots at all. It can fall asunder like a glassware any time when one of the members of the family goes astray. But the misbehaviour of one of its members alone wouldn't affect the integrity of the family. Do you know why I am telling you all these?' Mildred threw a poser to Maxwell.

'Mom, I don't know, but tell me why,' Maxwell asked like a submissive lamb.

'It's just because you're young and have a long way to go to understand all these,' Mildred said.

'But, Mom, you didn't tell me how the integrity could be kept intact by the other members of the family when a member of it misbehaves?' Maxwell wanted an explanation from his mother on that point.

'Even if one of the members of the family misbehaves, the others of the family can make adjustments, keeping in view the integrity of the family and preventing it from falling apart. You don't have to go elsewhere to learn all these. You have your own experience from our own family. It's just because of our patience and perseverance our family is intact. I could have very well left him or you could have left the family for some distant job prospects than pursuing your studies under a father whose ways are unreliable,' Mildred said.

Maxwell had nothing to say against his mother when she cited the example of their own family. But the thought of him leaving his mother for distant job prospects suddenly came up in his mind, which disturbed him no end.

'That will never be . . .,' his disturbed mind asserted. Then he thought, 'My mother has more wisdom than me. It could be her experiments with life under a wayward husband that made her wise and knowledgeable. She could fend for herself even in my absence. She has more sense. She is more tactical than anybody else to tackle a foolhardy husband.' Maxwell thought to console his own mind.

'What I feel is now you're getting ready for an unnecessary showdown by questioning father. Why do you go for all these? Your question would only help him get flared up. Why you create bad blood? You should have a concern for your own future. As I told, you have to make adjustments, avoiding embarrassing questions that would provoke father. It's this kind of adjustments I want from you now. You know how much I adjust. Many of the situations that would have caused an explosion in our family went off quietly. Then it's just as well you must not do anything that would make your own future uncertain. Don't forget you're still a dependent on your father.' Mildred showed more wisdom than her volatile son.

'Anyway, Mom, I can't help asking Father the reasons for his such strange habits. How long can we suppress our inquisitiveness?' Maxwell said again, not able to prevent himself from asking.

Mildred could ascribe his attitude only to his youthful inexperience and adamantine nature. She thought his attitude was a foolhardy one. She was more concerned about avoiding such a meeting between the father and son.

'If you're so bent upon knowing the reason, I think it's not you but me who should be the best person to ask him. I think I would be more diplomatic,' Mildred suggested. Even as she offered to ask, she was apprehensive of its consequences and it's yielding a positive result; there was the probability of her mission failing with her stubborn husband and the probability of his bashing her at the slightest provocation for which she knew she had to be extra cautious and careful. She could not ever forget her past – the wounds her husband had inflicted in her mind for no fault of hers in so many similar situations. His unpredictable nature was always a threat to her and the family. But she adjusted for the sake of the family, for its integrity.

'Mom, if you feel it's the safest method it's okay for me. But you should be certain to bring him round to tell the real reason,' Maxwell said.

The last part of his words: 'You should be certain to bring him round to tell the real reason', made Mildred certain that if a direct confrontation between the father and the son was allowed, it would end up in yet another quarrel because she could realize well in advance the serious undertones to her son's innocuous request to her and its ensuing undesirable consequences. His emphasis on the words 'certain' and 'the real reason' meant he wouldn't be satisfied with a make-believe or evasive reply from his father.

The talk between the mother and son didn't give peace of mind to Mildred. The undertone of the talk was disquieting to her. But it was a consolation for her that Maxwell had agreed to her talking to her husband on behalf of him.

Days passed.

Chapter 7

It was a Sunday morning. A sleeping Rodrigues showed signs of waking up. But soon he lapsed into moments of some spiritual thoughts, which was unusual of him. 'Fantasies are the fleeting wishful thoughts of an empty mind. But a mind that believes is filled to satiety with immeasurable grace of God. It's the grace of God that makes a believer soulful, which sustains him that way. All believers are bestowed with this legacy from God. As a believer, soul is the source of my life. If I'm soulless, I would be as good as a corpse. And so is the case with any non-believer. My firm belief makes me the chosen disciple of the Goddess of Naga, who inspires and exalts my senses to a higher level of spiritual enlightenment. One who reaches this sensitive and receptive stage of spiritual enlightenment could rightly sense the wishes of the goddess. It's a rare kind of spiritual intuition that works. Any believer who reaches this level could share the thoughts of God and rightly interpret them. And this is how I could discern what all are the wishes of the goddess and what all aren't,' Rodrigues soliloquised.

'God never speaks directly to the believer. But he eloquently converses with him through signs, symbols, and revelations in the form of dreams on how to conduct himself the God's way. And it's incumbent on any believer to carry out such wishes diligently,' Rodrigues mused.

It was one such revelation of the goddess that gave birth to a secret yearning in his mind some time ago for its fruition. It was something which he never liked to share with any. It had a significant bearing on his belief in the Goddess of Naga and his Naga descent, which, he believed, would make his present more meaningful and promising when carried out. And he waited patiently for the right moment. But to him the right moment wasn't a future point of time when he would be in a better disposition. He hadn't such expectations. He never dreamt of something like a prosperous future to come upon him because he was one to whom the future held no charm. A man of wayward habits, future to him always looked lustreless and bleak. It wasn't something for him to pin any hope on. To him, it was something fraught with a kind of uncertain anticipation, a kind of vague promises, a kind of misplaced contemplation, a kind of extravagant presumptions based on unrealistic expectations and unsure assurances. His unsure ways of life made him think so. He viewed the Goddess of Naga as his only saviour, as somebody for him to fall back upon. At times, he would look within, and every time he could unmistakably find out that he was a reckless man of undesirable, wayward ways. He believed the goddess would pardon his sins as her firm believer. He always believed his Naga descent made him a different entity. Looking back, he saw the blessings of the Goddess of Naga to him in abundance – its ethereal enormous glow from the past that highlighted his very existence in the present. He believed the blessings came to him from his past and not from the dismal present or bleak future, anyway. So he always dreamt of his past – of those glorious, blessed bygone days of his linear ascendants, their belief, their happiness, their bliss, their contentment and jubilation that drowned them in a rare kind of ethereal, dreamy ecstasy and pride. He wanted to imbibe and put into practice their experience, their happy disposition, which they were in. He believed they were better off than him.

Rodrigues once again thought of the significance of the act, which the goddess wanted him to do. And the very thought triggered a bubbling spirit in him, which couldn't be doused until its fruition. So he kept in his mind the big idea as his dream, as his marvellous enlightenment, as his benign duty for him to be carried out for sure. But still his mind wasn't at rest, or he couldn't put it to rest either. The desire grew taller and taller, stronger and stronger, bigger and bigger. Time passed, not waiting for any. Meanwhile, so many strong symbolic thoughts of his dream passed through his mind, which day by day developed into an uncanny obsession powerful than himself in his mind. Even then he never wanted to share it with his wife and son, who had been kept in the dark for long with boggled minds.

Chapter 8

And then came the day . . ., when something happened which surprised the mother and the son no end. Rodrigues called the mother and son and said that he wanted to tell them something. They guessed a revelation was soon to take place. They couldn't ascribe any other reason for Rodrigues's sudden volte-face in his attitude towards them. They waited expectantly for something exciting . . .

Then he opened up. Instead of plunging directly into the central point of the secret, he started from its periphery so that he could slowly unfurl the entire secret to his wife and son.

'I can't help viewing these termitaries on the walls with awe and reverence. The termitaries and the overgrown creepers on our house are a fine symbolic blend that gives our house the looks of a sacred place, the halo of a snake-shrine. But I know it's not so for you. The Goddess of Naga has enshrined it. Its sanctity, its holiness, and its blessedness are nothing but the handiwork of the Goddess of Naga.' He once again reminisced, 'My forefathers were from the north-eastern part of India. They were Nagas who worshipped the snakes, and it was thus they came to be known as Nagas. And you know, it's from here my pedigree started. They were converts into Christianity at the instance of the British missionary. But still they maintained their traditional belief and worship of Naga, and this was how I'm a Christian now and a follower of Naga belief.'

Maxwell and Mildred received his revelation with mixed emotions. The Naga ancestry of Rodrigues was news to Mildred and Maxwell. Rodrigues had successfully kept this a secret from Mildred before and after their marriage. When Maxwell was born, such details lost their significance. And they lived on . . .

'And I tell you, I'm going to install a snake shrine in our courtyard soon, which would bring my dream to reality. Two priests are coming to visit our house for the installation ceremony,' Rodrigues put his revelations in a nutshell because he didn't want to elaborate.

'Isn't it a kind of double speak? Something like sailing in two boats at the same time?' Maxwell retorted, who couldn't swallow his father's view.

'It's none of your business,' Mildred cut in, with a new wave of energy. His mother's sudden volte-face surprised him no end. He felt his mother's words were tinted with a bit of aggressiveness, which was unusual of her.

Mildred too felt her answer was a little bit hasty and harsh, and she regretted instantly. It was her overwhelming fear of an ensuing altercation between the father and son, which she always wanted to avoid for the sake of her own son, that made her talk in that fashion.

'Why, Mother?! Aren't you a Christian, a believer in Jesus Christ? You have no Naga ancestry to boast. You aren't an idol worshipper. You often speak to me so. And now what makes you support this kind of superstitions?' Maxwell asked in surprise, gently putting his arm around her neck.

'I'm all that. But talk of such things is a waste. Now can't you be satisfied, at last your father has let out to you the secret behind his love for the termitaries and creepers, putting an end to all our speculations and guesswork once, for all?' Mildred, sensing a father–son confrontation, was trying to avoid it.

'But can't I express my opinion even if it is different from my father's?' Maxwell spoke in a low voice.

'You can very well express your opinion even if it's different from your father's,' Mildred said.

'But now didn't I do the same thing only? Then why do you find fault with me?' Maxwell spoke, a little surprised.

'Yes, but you expressed your opinion at the inopportune time. And it was this that I opposed,' Mildred clarified . . .

'Mom, I can't agree with your opinion. To me it's not an inopportune time,' Maxwell opined.

'But still you should have pulled yourself, instead of blurting out your opposing views. You must not let loose your mind. Now do I have to remind you this off and on when only you would be reticent? When only you would have the sense of propriety? When only you would speak wisdom?' Mildred asked.

'You mean I should express my opinion diplomatically?' Maxwell asked.

'Diplomacy is always good. But I feel you're not going to gain anything even if you're diplomatic,' Mildred said. The talk ended there.

Mildred's support was a blessing in disguise for Rodrigues. But it was double-edged, for the sake of domestic peace and more importantly for the sake of Maxwell's future well-being. That was the reason that she took an opposing stand against Maxwell.

Maxwell's talk would have normally aroused his volatile father. But strangely he was calm.

'It may sound double speak. But it's experience really. You know experience is the best teacher. But to learn from experience, one has to be observant over so many years. And you have just passed your teens and have a long way to go to gather experience. So you won't understand. Worshiping Naga (snake) brings prosperity. And anyone who gives up Naga worship would unwittingly bring bad times in his life. One of my ancestors, after changing into Christianity, gave up Naga worship. And calamities befell his family. It's believed wherever a person with Naga ancestry was, he would be subjected to the wrath of the Goddess of Naga, if he forsook his Naga belief. Then it would be hell for him,' Rodrigues cautioned him.

Mildred too nodded in assent to what her husband said. But this was usual, as it was done for the sake of domestic peace. But it had the least impact upon their son, Maxwell, who was not carried away by the apprehension of calamity or the vanity of heredity. He left such things to his parents to boast of. He was more interested in his own world of friends and studies. Days wore off. Then something happened . . .

Chapter 9

On a holiday morning, Maxwell saw his father coming home with two strangers.

'Look, Mom, here comes Dad with two others,' Maxwell said.

Mildred came out. They were strangers.

One looked like a Hindu priest. The other one was in his teens. He looked like the assistant of the priest. Their very looks agreed yet betrayed disagreement and discordance in some other aspects. Their foreheads and chests bore lines of sacred sandalwood paste. On their foreheads were big round dots of red, made of *kumkum* powder. Their heads were tonsured. A holy thread of white ran across the torso of each, from the right shoulder to the left flank, the knotted end of which went down below the waistline of their dhotis. The younger one, carrying a bundle, ragged because of long usage, was lean and of medium height.

'I brought them to set up the snake shrine,' Rodrigues said, introducing them to his wife and son.

'But you didn't tell me of their visit today in advance?' Mildred asked, slightly embarrassed.

The reason for her embarrassment was that she hadn't been able to make special food as was usual when guests called on a family. In such cases, it was the worry of the mistress of the house to ply the guests with different varieties of tasty food.

'That's no problem. We could make do with what we have. And they are of simple food habits,' Rodrigues replied, giving her confidence.

'Now, where is it to be installed?' Mildred asked, slightly apprehensive that the place of installation and the place she had in her mind to set up a vegetable garden might coincide. Rodrigues sensed the purpose of her question. So he got a little irritated. Maxwell was, as usual, indifferent.

'Wherever it is, it's none of your business to fix the spot. It's that of the priest . . . See, you can't set up a snake shrine wherever you want. There are certain divine laws governing the selection of the place. The priest would look into the positions of certain planets and stars – the eastern, western, southern, northern directions, and make certain astrological calculations before fixing the point. And one can't expect it to be at a particular place according to one's convenience. If it could be fixed anywhere according to our wish and convenience, there is no need to depend on astrology. Then there is no need of a priest. Then the place cannot be called a shrine. Do you think just fixing an idol somewhere in our premises is our purpose?' Rodrigues replied, showing his full agreement with the priest's choice of the place of installation.

'It's not my business or your business. But what the heck if I asked? I didn't say the shrine should be installed at a particular place, according to my convenience,' Mildred replied, slightly offended.

'But you should understand we aren't to decide the place,' Rodrigues said.

'I know it,' Mildred replied.

'You must know this is an auspicious moment,' Rodrigues said.

'Yes, I know it too,' Mildred replied.

'You must know it's a consecration that's going to take place,' Rodrigues said.

'I know that also,' Mildred said.

'I know why you asked the question. You're worried if the installation would be on the place that you have in your mind for your vegetable garden,' Rodrigues said.

'Yes, but so what?' Mildred asked.

'If it's the place where the priest finds most suitable, it would be selected. Your vegetable garden has only secondary importance. Then one should not entertain any other thought on such a solemn occasion. It will spoil the sanctity of the moment,' Rodrigues said.

Normally, this situation would have made Rodrigues throw a tantrum. But strangely, he looked a changed man. The reason could be his over-riding thought not to spoil the sanctity of the situation.

'No time to waste on inanities. So hurry up. And it's not proper to make someone wait for another. The day's forecast says the auspicious moment is soon to start. If we miss it, we will have to bring the priest again, which is a sheer waste of time and energy, so no question of missing it. Now it's time to get ready,' Rodrigues urged.

Everyone got ready and moved to the spot of the priest's choice.

The assistant priest had to set up certain articles in their proper places for the ceremony. He opened his bundle in utmost veneration and took out some articles. One was a handbell made of bronze. The others were some red flowers of hibiscus, a packet of camphor, and a small bronze lamp. He filled the lamp with coconut oil and lit it. He spread a dhoti before the place to be consecrated, leaving a space of three feet between the sanctum and the spread dhoti for a bonfire. Then he piled up a small heap of sandalwood splinters. All other paraphernalia were placed in their proper places on the dhoti. He fixed a replica of three snakes chiselled in one granite piece on the sanctum. Then he set fire to the heap of sandalwood splinters . . . Rodrigues and Mildred waited devoutly for the auspicious moment to get underway. But Maxwell wasn't that keen.

The priest looked at Rodrigues. His eyes were half closed in veneration. His face sported a strange look – a kind of calmness and a strange glaze writ large on his face. Then as if he had lost his tongue for a few minutes, he gestured to Rodrigues, his wife, and son to move closer to him. The atmosphere was calm and serene. Not a word was exchanged; not a whisper was heard. Once again, he looked at Rodrigues. It was to signify that the ceremony was soon to start. Rodrigues nodded in assent. Everyone stood in rapt attention, ready to receive the shower of blessings. As Mildred had a Penchant for music her mind was more set on hearing a melodious hymn than the rites performed on the occasion. So with great expectations she waited. But Rodrigues' thoughts were solely fixed on the snake goddess's blessings. Maxwell was apathetic.

The priest and his assistant squatted in front of the dhoti. The assistant caught hold of the hand-bell. Then as if the priest had regained his voice, he burst into a sudden chanting of mantras at the top of his voice. The assistant too joined him, a little later. This caused their chanting to sound a little out of phase. There was discordance in their pitch too. There was glaring mismatch in all respects and aspects of a good rendition of the hymns. No one could help it. Mildred was sad and frustrated. It was as if the musician in her had got a punch in the face. The shaking of the bell was not at all in conformity with the strains and rhythm of the mantras. It had an aura of sadness, as it was in a slow, melancholic rhythm, more akin to the tolling of bells in a funeral procession. From a distance, the function seemed like a musical concert of crows – a hotchpotch of noise. Meanwhile, the priest threw the hibiscus flowers thrice, which fell scattered on the deity and all over the place to be consecrated. This was followed by the priest throwing the camphor crystals into the fire, which rekindled the bonfire. Each time he threw the camphor, the fire stood up with a hissing and searing sound. The hissing frightened the fowls and chickens reared by Mildred, and they flew away for their dear lives, cackling. Then he sprinkled some water and started blowing a *makidi*, the one used by the snake charmers, closing his eyes to show extreme piety to the Goddess of Naga. Everyone was fervently praying, their eyes closed, for the blessings and good times to come upon them. Maxwell was indifferent, but he had to keep his protest to himself. He was amused for a moment when he saw the chickens flying away in panic. A few solemn moments of calm and confidence passed. A breeze from nowhere wafted around, making the dry leaves rustle for a few minutes, and then subsided, as if a harbinger of something untoward to happen. Then something like a hissing sound was heard followed by the unusual rustle of dry leaves on the ground, when there was actually no wind to stir them. The assistant of the priest thought the priest was hissing out the dry phlegm from his nostrils, lest it should cause him to sneeze while chanting the mantras. But the priest thought the same with his assistant. Hearing that sound again made the priest and the assistant open their eyes, and to their shock, they saw a real snake with its hood spread, dancing to the tunes of the *makidi*. At the unexpected sight of a live snake, the priest and his assistant struggled to be on to their feet and jumped aback in sudden reflex. The bell in the hands of the assistant shivered involuntarily. Soon the priest got rid of his initial embarrassment and spoke. 'Lo! The Naga goddess has materialized before us in the form of a real snake. All of you don't panic. And believe me, wherever I went to set up a snake shrine, it was the usual sight. It signified that the Goddess of Naga was placated,' he said. Everyone saw a cobra with its hood spread, which appeared as if from nowhere. It was a surprise to all. The snake soon slithered away. Then some milk and a plantain fruits were placed before the deity. The sudden crowing of a crow was heard from the branch of a nearby tree. It was slanting its head in different angles as if due to sudden reflexes. The priest felt no difficulty in explaining that the crow was the embodiment of the Goddess of Naga too in its yet another incarnation and that it had come to eat the plantain fruit and shower its blessings on all of them. Once the function was over and everyone was leaving the spot to have their breakfast, they saw the crow suddenly darting off the tree and pecking at the plantain fruit in one scoop; it flew back and settled on the same branch and started gorging on it. After breakfast, the priest gave them some instructions on how to maintain the holy place. 'Let the lamp at the sanctum be lit. Let it be regular. Let there be trees and shrubs. Let them proliferate too. Let there be grass. Let them grow wild too. Let there be wind to put out the lamp. And let the lamp outlive it. Let there be a cloudburst to douse the lamp. And let the lamp outlive it too. Let there be the blessings in abundance of the Goddess of Naga upon the family. Let the blessings be everlasting too.'

'Did you all understand what is conveyed by the blessings?' the priest asked.

'No, but what's the big idea?' Rodrigues and Mildred asked.

'The winds and the cloudburst are the embodiment of evil spirits to take away the blessings from your family. The lamp is symbolic of your family's blessings. And if the winds and the cloudburst are not able to douse the light, what does it mean? It means none could take away the blessings and protections offered to your family by the Goddess of Naga,' the priest assured them.

After the breakfast, the priest avidly watched Rodrigues's movement in great expectation. His morose face had a sudden glow, which couldn't be doused by anything on earth, when Rodrigues handed out to him an envelope which he knew contained his fees.

The priest readily accepted it. Soon they left.

Chapter 10

On his way back, the assistant asked the priest, 'Why you told them, "Wherever you went to set up a snake shrine, a real snake would appear"? I'm the only person who used to accompany you on such occasions. But this is the first time when a real snake appeared.'

'Shut up! You aren't grown tall enough to question the God,' the priest burst out scornfully.

'I'm not questioning the Almighty. I'm asking you some clarifications about what you said to clear my doubts,' the assistant said politely.

'My authority as a priest is a traditional sacred legacy from the Goddess of Naga. And I'm directly linked with the goddess. And my interpretations are godly. No one can question them. Such blasphemous questions to me would be as good as questioning the goddess and her ways. And what I say and do are by virtue of my authority from the goddess, to sustain the belief of the people in the goddess. Yes, it's my duty . . . It's my bounden duty . . . to keep the belief of the disciples untampered. My interpretations of events may be frilled,I mean some deviations from truth, to make a belief more believable. But it's the purpose that justifies frilling. As a priest, it's my duty to keep the belief of the believers intact and be instrumental in handing down the belief to generations. This is the way to spread the message of the goddess,' the priest expostulated with an air of vehemence. 'You don't have the call of the goddess, even after your two years' learning in the monastery.'

'I agree. But isn't frilling a lie, a sin, when a priest is bound to speak truth?' the assistant asked, confused.

'Mind you, frilling is not a lie when it comes to belief. There's no proof for any kind of belief. So belief, its sanctity, solemnity, and spirituality have to be protected through suitable interpretations. Then only it could be everlasting. It's the bounden duty of believers, especially people like us, to spread the belief at any cost to eternalise belief. It's by vigilant protection that belief could assume immortality and eternity. A belief without frilling is a dead duck, soon to fall into oblivion. Every religion allows frilling. When it is difficult to prove a belief, resorting to frilling is not a sin. And frilling in this context is a kind of tempering a belief believable beyond any doubt. It's the purpose that matters. If belief can be fixed only with the help of frilling, there is no harm in resorting to it. The faith in the goddess is our traditional sacred belief. And we should have implicit faith in our belief. Doubts have no place in a believer's mind. The belief of a wavering mind would give rise to doubts. But a strong mind with firm belief wouldn't waver and then no doubt would crop up in the mind. In such situations, frilling is an aiding factor – some fabrications, some twisting, or distortion of facts to make the belief beyond doubt,' the priest expostulated. His assistant's silence made him happy. The priest secretly gloated at his success in silencing his assistant. But his happiness was short-lived.

'But couldn't it be a stray snake that came our way during the consecration?' the assistant asked, slightly apprehensive of earning the wrath of the priest . . .

'Couldn't as well the snake that appeared on the spot be the embodiment of the Goddess of Naga? How could you assert it's not but a stray one? Isn't the possibility fifty–fifty?' the priest countered.

'If that was so, shouldn't a snake appear at each and every installation ceremony wherever we set up snake shrines?' the assistant asked.

'You jerk! You will never learn, you senseless, silly idiot!' hissed the priest.

'Guruji, don't misunderstand me. I'm asking these questions to make my belief intact, to alley my doubts by your cogent answers,' the assistant answered, embarrassed by the priest's rude reply. His answer had an air of flattery to bring the priest round to an amicable mood.

'Didn't I tell you about frilling?' the priest repeated as if to remind his assistant, who seemed to be not satisfied by his answer.

'Yes, Guruji,' the assistant said.

'Tell me, what did it mean?' the priest asked.

'Some small deviations from truth are okay to keep the disciples' belief intact,' the assistant answered.

'A priest or for that matter all the priests are under a bounden duty to uphold their belief to make others believe in what they preach. This is more an objective method. How far you are able to convince the believers is what counts more than how far you're able to convince yourself. But your belief in what you preach is significant in the sense that it is an aiding factor as far as the spreading of belief to others is concerned. As a priest, one is duty bound to spread the belief to as many as possible. And for that, you have to use frilling wherever it's needed to make the belief professed by you believable beyond any doubt. Belief is something that cannot be proved. But it can be established by frilling. Then only the belief could sustain in this world. Then only religions could sustain in this world. Belief is a vast ocean that has engulfed truth. This is so because finding the truth of all the belief is an impossibility. Here comes in the significance of frilling. And frilling in this context assumes a noble role and does a noble job to establish a great belief like the belief in God believable. And for that matter, even in cases of truth, frilling comes to the rescue in establishing a truth. It's in cases when evidence alone cannot prove truth. And just as there are truth in this world supported by frilling, belief too can be sustained through frilling,' the priest replied.

'Guruji, could you give me an example when frilling is needed to establish a truth?' The assistant was at the peak of his inquisitiveness.

'Sometimes truth is one thing and the evidence is against truth. This happens in a court of law. The accused may be innocent. But the evidence to prove his innocence may not be there. Then frilling comes into play. Here the frilling is made use of by the lawyer of the accused to prove truth. Here frilling assumes a noble role,' said the priest who had a stint as a lawyer for two years before joining the monastery.

'And for that matter, I'll tell you something more . . .

The roots of belief are in its antiquity – its unquestioned faith handed down to generations after generations. Our bounden duty as priests is to propagate belief. God has selected us and entrusted with us this noble role to be carried out. That is why we are priests. That's why not all people are priests. And that makes us different from ordinary mortals. This makes our status in the society unique. And that's why the believers throng around us for their religious needs. Belief is just as well trusting your faith firmly: If you firmly order a hill to move away, it would move away. But take it from me, "doubting Thomases" like you can never perform this feat,' the priest added.

The assistant wasn't fully convinced. So he had one more question to ask the priest. He struggled to calm his mind – to hush it up. But he couldn't help asking the priest. His mental make-up was never to swallow something put into his mouth. He couldn't help dissecting them to find out if they were edible to him. He could never ignore the absence of logic. So a question darted out of his mouth once again despite all his efforts to leave the priest alone.

'Guruji, I saw you moving aback with a start on seeing the snake. Why was it so?' the assistant asked diffidently.

The priest knew suddenly that angry words would not do with people like him. So he was calm this time.

'It was my respect to the goddess from whom I got the legacy of my priesthood and who brought us all welfare. It was not at all an expression of any fear but my awe and reverence,' the priest replied in a polite manner, expecting his answer would settle his doubts.

But it was not to be. He was up with yet another question.

" Guruji you never seemed to be awestricken , you never moved aback with a start when you saw the crow"

Going by your words, the crow that had appeared on the scene was none other than the soul of the Goddess of Naga,' the assistant asked discreetly, so as not to provoke the priest.

All these time, the priest was thinking of how to silence his assistant. He knew he couldn't beat about the bush but had to be to the point. So he gave him a piece of his mind.

'A crow and a snake are different. Naturally, when we see a snake you think of it as a ferocious creature. But a crow can never be ferocious. So the difference in my response may be due to this factor,' the priest replied, half admitting.

'So you don't much believe in what you told everybody that the snake was the embodiment of the Goddess of Naga? If the snake was surely the embodiment of the Goddess of Naga, why must you think of its ferocity? Why must you be afraid of it?' the assistant asked.

The priest was in a blind alley. But soon an answer came to his rescue to stop further questions from the assistant.

'I'm going to tell the high priest about your doubts and questions and would recommend yet another two more years of training for you in the monastery,' the priest answered nonchalantly.

But his answer clicked. The assistant thought disgustingly of his spending yet another two more years in the prison-like monastery, which he wanted to avoid at any cost.

'Guruji, I will not ask any more questions if only you could spare me yet another term in the monastery . . .

Enough is enough,' the assistant submitted meekly.

'Then don't do anything that invites the wrath of the goddess, I tell you,' the priest replied in a reconciling mood, at once happy and relieved that he had succeeded in silencing his assistant, though in an evasive manner.

Chapter 11

Rodrigues was all contentment. He felt as if he had carried out his pious obligation to the Goddess of Naga. Life for Rodrigues moved on as usual. He would reach home from work in the evening, his feet barely touching the ground. Then he would straightaway go to the dining room and fall onto his favourite dining chair by the window, enjoying the gusts of wind from the backwaters that smelt of fish and salt, crooning over and again his favourite number coined by him, praising his unending passion for his drunken experience, till food was served on the table. He sang in a raucous, strident voice with a heavy tongue. Everyone who heard him sing never wanted him to sing any more. Nevertheless, he went on singing and the members of his family had to suffer a lot.

> *I want the fire water*
> *More and more,*
> *That caresses, swings,*
> *Sways and swirls,*
> *Keeping me afloat, like*
> *A rolling vessel in the backwaters.*

'Tell your mom to bring me something to eat. I'm hungry,' he demanded when he saw Maxwell.

'Your stomach is already full. Then how could you be hungry?' Maxwell who could never appreciate his father's drunken habits showed his dislike.

'You know, I'm the master of this house. You're not supposed to pick on your father in this fashion,' Rodrigues, with his eyes half closed, replied indistinctly, wagging his heavy tongue.

'But you aren't father-like to me?. You aren't husband-like to my mother. You're a wife basher. Aren't you an irresponsible and superstitious person, not at all deserving to be called a father or a husband?' Maxwell asked.

'But don't forget I earn. I eke out a living for the family. I fund your education, and what more do you want?' Rodrigues grumbled.

'You earn. But not for your family but to waste on your pleasures. You bring home some pittance. And even your funding my education is precarious. No one can predict when you will stop it. You're unreliable. Once you warned me you would stop paying for my education. So you're not to speak much about your largesse,' Maxwell said.

'You thankless bastard! Yes, now I realize it's high time you earned yourself. I joined the distillery and started earning when I was twenty. But you're still a shameless dependent on me at twenty-three. You're an extra in my house. And I would warn you, this kind of cavalier nature would spoil your chances,' Rodrigues spoke in a threatening tone.

To this, Maxwell didn't reply as if he was suddenly reminded of his mother's advice. He realized he had blurted out something which he shouldn't have made, seeing the gravity of the insinuation in his father's talk. He regretted his thoughtlessness.

'I should have pulled myself. I have to play it safe if I'm to push on for one more year for my degree in education and then till I fetch a teacher's job. Yes, I'm still a dependent on my father. So I shouldn't do anything that would embarrass him. Yes, I have to keep him in good humour for my own sake.' The thought resounded in his ears like an echo of his mother's advice.

Mildred heard the talk between the father and son and was sad. She couldn't find words to stop her husband and son. She knew the only way to divert her husband before things got worse was to bring the food on the table. While serving the food, she looked at Maxwell with compassion and a kind of regret at the harsh words of her husband. But the father was still arrogant and looked unrelenting, murmuring some curses intermittently like the aftershock of an earthquake. The altercation between the father and the son roused in Mildred an intense anxious expectation of something bad to happen. Her sad look at Maxwell suddenly aroused in him, once again, foreboding thoughts, and he sensed the disquieting undertones in his father's talk. He feared that his father wouldn't hesitate to do what he had told him. He knew those words were not the outbursts of an angry father who would soon cool down and regret later and turn compassionate. Mildred noticed a strong detestation in the eyes of her son, though he looked helpless and regretting. She feared if further provoked, her son's detestation would boom out into an eruption against his father any time.

'In this family, I'm the trouble-shooter and similar situations would make my task difficult,' Mildred thought.

The alcohol in his stomach had worked up his appetite. When he finished, he stood up staggeringly and kicked off the chair which had supported him so far. Mildred knew it was an expression of his extreme anger towards his son that still lingered in his mind. Turning to Mildred, he said, 'Tell your

son I'm his father. I'm the master of this house. Don't forget .
.. Don't forget . . . Yes, don't forget. Tell him, tell him . . .'

He moved to his bed, crooning his favourite number in a
more indistinct manner. His voice slowly tapered into a
whisper, and falling on to the bed he was soon asleep.

After the incident, an anxious Mildred called her son aside
and beseeched, 'Don't spoil your future by provoking father. I
have told you, you should show more sagacity and wisdom to
be patient. You ought not to have provoked him. He only told
you to tell me to bring food. But you provoked him
unnecessarily. Your reply to your father wasn't the way one
should talk to one's father. I think I need not have to remind
you off and on that you have some more distance to go before
you are free from the clutches of your father. And I tell you,
this time it is your fault to provoke him when you should be
doing something to avoid a confrontation.'

'But, Mom, sometimes our acts may be impulsive and our
talk momentary. Isn't it natural? Isn't it part of human
behaviour?' Maxwell talked in a philosophical vein. It was a
kind of rationalisation on his part to justify his thoughtless
outbursts at his father for which he regretted internally.

'But you aren't a kid to blurt out something. You should
be on your guard,' Mildred said.

'But it's possible to people like you only. You have a life
of long suffering. It must have taught you lessons. But I haven't
such a long experience. Then is he father-like to me? I'm not
talking about the present situation but the so many situations
over the years. Is father–son relationship one–way traffic?
Mom, I can't be convinced by your reasoning,' added Maxwell,
not fully recovered from his angry mood. 'Maxy, you could

very well have avoided the present incident. But I know your provoking behaviour was a sudden outburst of your pent-up feeling of the neglect you suffered from your father, but for which I don't see any reason for you to get provoked. But don't think I'm not talking logic or that I'm sitting in judgement. In your present condition, it's not logic of any kind, but practical thinking that works. You talk sense and your father talks nonsense. But on some occasions, one has to accept nonsense for practical purposes. I want you to be a gainer in your tussle with your father because I love you. You have a bright future and I want to ensure it for you. But you must know that sometimes it's not discordance but concordance that brings glory in your life. It's not highhandedness but little bit of submissiveness on your part that works for your good. You have to be consistent. I tell you, you aren't to make things worse for you by your impulsive, thoughtless outbursts,' Mildred said.

When Mildred said this, Maxwell noticed a strange glow, a glint of hope still on her sad face. It was the hope of a loving mother that her son would mend his ways.

'Mom, what you said is absolutely correct. Now I feel extreme contrition. I shouldn't have provoked Father. What I did was a kind of onslaught on my father when he didn't tell me anything to provoke me. He was just telling me to tell you he wanted food. And I should have passed that information to you, which I didn't. You love me. You hope for a bright future for me. I should have realized it. But I was thoughtless. I didn't take your advice seriously to pull myself. It was due to the prejudice my father had caused in my mind over the years and his continuing to be so even now that prompted me to misbehave with him. And I'm sorry now. When he was home, you had to wait in anxious expectation of his blows. But you were tactfully submissive. I should have taken you as a model for my conduct when I dealt with Father. What you said is correct. I should have shown sagacity and wisdom and kept myself within my limits. And I realize a wrong prejudicial move on my part towards Father affects you more and makes you more chagrined. It brings you added frustration if my father does something in pursuance of his warning to me,' Maxwell told his mother regretfully.

'Your father would adopt any method that occurs to his perverted mind, if he is provoked. This you have to bear in mind. You have to be cautious when you deal with the likes of your father,' Mildred gave him a final advice.

'Mom! You're not only my mother but an angel guide, who can only wish well for me in my life, who guides me through the right path, who guards me from the travails and tribulations in my life. I want you to be always with me, even when I pass out and get a job and settle in my life. Wherever I'm, you should be with me. It's only a question of some more time as you very well know.' Maxwell turned emotional as he said these words.

'But I can't fully endorse your view. Don't forget the basic thing that your father, me, and you make our family. The pleasure of family life, with all its drawbacks, is something unique. I mean the feeling of togetherness, the sense of belonging, and all that cannot be ignored. And then it's the bounden duty of each one of us to contribute his share towards that goal. Now I can only say you cannot ignore these factors,' Mildred philosophized.

'But to tame Father is something impossible. What do you say?' Maxwell asked, waiting for her reply.

'Son, you have to think of the essential goodness in man and work for that. Success will be yours. I haven't lost any hope about your father, because the goodness in man is infectious. And if our behaviour is good, it could make your father good too. Good behaviour gives out the fragrance of unity. If our behaviour is one of tolerance, I'm sure your father too couldn't help assimilating it. The fragrance of good behaviour is a panacea that would treat your father to become good. It requires persistence, perseverance, and sustenance on our part. It's not one or two days' affair. Fight it to the last and that should be our refrain. That should be our watchword. It doesn't mean you should swallow father's wayward ways. You have the right to protest. You have the right to make him known that you don't accept a trait or traits in your father's character. Then only he can review his conduct and mend his ways. By our good conduct, we're giving Father an opportunity to rethink, even if a revamp may be a far cry.' Maxwell couldn't accept his mother's philosophy.

'Perversions are typical of a stubborn, unrelenting, and unreceptive mind that cannot be done away with that easily,' Maxwell thought. He couldn't accept his mother's philosophy, but he felt there was practical wisdom in her thoughts.

Days wore off.

Chapter 12

Rodrigues was happy. He believed he could at once placate the Goddess of Naga and his ancestors when he could successfully install a snake shrine in his courtyard. Maxwell had to submit to his father's wish. And for that matter, his mother too was in favour of it. The reasons that made Maxwell swallow his protest and made his mother support the installation were different. In fact, he was obliging his mother who supported his father's strange plans. But his mother's reason was to make family life peaceful by avoiding a confrontation between the father and son. But none could subscribe to Rodrigues's view of pleasing the Goddess of Naga and his ancestors, which they knew was superstitious.

'And for that matter, my father alone was responsible for the presence of a snake shrine in our courtyard, and we're condemned to submit meekly to his wishes,' Maxwell told his mother to which she didn't reply, but she was thoughtful, a strange, untold, pathetic look of glum writ large on her face. Maxwell couldn't understand the meaning of it.

Days rolled on uneventfully. But worse was to come.

Chapter 13

Once Rodrigues, Mike, and Hibson were having their usual boozing session. They all were enjoying the free quota of liquor allowed by their employer Ramsay to his employees.

'Our employer is a good soul. If we aren't allowed the free quota, we would have been brokes, having had to spend the entire money needed from our own pockets,' Rodrigues opined gratefully.

Hibson, who was always the one who did the most grumbling among the lot, in his fully lit-up condition, took strong exceptions to Rodrigues's opinion.

'It's none of his largesse. I would have agreed with you if he hadn't put an upper limit for the quota. We all know his quota is nothing, considering our need for liquor. If he really loves us, why does he put an upper limit to our quota? The state has fixed a quota of alcohol for each *Abkari*. But don't you know he smuggles alcohol from other states in excess of his state fixed quota for a lesser price? And to double his profits that way?. He is cunning. He has an ulterior aim for his kindly gesture. He needs our cooperation in his illegal business of selling hooch. So he wants to keep us in good humour,' Hibson protested.

'If we are employed elsewhere, we would have been brokes, paying for our lavish drink binges. Now we could as well find some extra money for our sustenance,' Rodrigues observed again.

'We must thank our employer for what he does for us. He never interferes with our boozing sessions. The only restriction is we shouldn't drink during duty time,' Mike, one of Rodrigues's colleagues, agreed with Rodrigues.

'But then we won't be takers daily, as it's today. Every man can get attuned to his circumstances, a kind of adaptation. This is nature's law.' Hibson again took exception.

'But you can't generalize like that. Haven't you seen people drink beyond their means, leaving the members of his family to starve? Wasn't Jerrome of that type? He never had time even to go home. He used to drink late in the night and slept in the tavern itself,' Mike interrupted Hibson, using a specific example.

'In a way, we're lucky we are employed here. We don't have to go out visiting taverns for our drinks,' Rodrigues opined, expressing his gratitude to his employer once again.

'And we get pure, healthy stuff here. It gets us reasonably high. And what more do we need? And none will stand in our way if we want hooch,' Mike pointed out.

'The stuff we are supplied by our boss will never bite us back. If we have to go to our retail outlets, the story would be different. And we must be thankful to our boss.' Rodrigues too had a point.

They all loved drinks more than food.

'But the people want spurious stuff. They want to be high, as high as possible. They don't bother about the quality.' Mike turned the discussions to the people's attitude.

'Anyone who wants hooch can have it from our outlets and to his heart's content. There is no compulsion on the part of our employer that we should only drink the pure stuff supplied by him as our quota. We are free to choose. Isn't this a good trait of his character? Those who want to be more high can have hooch. If we feel we're fed nicely with pure stuff, why must we bother about our employer's surreptitious activities?' Rodrigues asked.

'It's a kind of blessing in disguise. If people wanted pure stuff only, the story would have been different,' Mike said with an air of apprehension. The sudden thought of his employer unable to pay the revenue to the government haunted him, if people wanted only the pure stuff.

'The *Abkaris* make good their loss by supplying cheap hooch which is much in need than pure stuff among labourers. The *Abkaris* can never make profit, even a reasonable one, by selling pure stuff alone. Then the business would be running at a heavy loss, leading them to bankruptcy. Then they will be forced to wind up their business. Soon the employees would be laid off,' Rodrigues soliloquised.

'Not only the taste of the drinking public is favourable, but the attitude of the Department of Revenue too is favourable,' Hibson expressed his view.

'But have you ever given a thought to the attitude of the government? If the ways of the revenue department are strange, the ways of the government are stranger. Those political leaders who man the governmental machinery and the revenue authorities and the police all love the *Abkaris*. They encourage the *Abkaris* to sell hooch in return for the gratifications they receive from them,' Mike revealed a known truth, once again for others to think over.

'What I feel is not only they but the drinking public too pave the way for such a malpractice to exist in our society. It's in a way violating the law intended to ward off evil from the society by encouraging these malpractices for our own self-aggrandisement. In fact, we are not to find fault with the government or the excise department or the police alone. Really, we all are responsible for the evil to sustain in our society,' Rodrigues opined.

'This is not an ignorable situation as you might think. It's a deadly evil that has deeply spread its roots in our society. As years pass, the roots go deeper and deeper. It brings in all sorts of evil to our society,' Mike revealed his apprehension of a potential danger that was going to engulf the society.

'Now leave it! Let us come to the concessions we enjoy here. No *Abkari* would ever be so kind to the employees as our master.' Rodrigues was all praise for and grateful to Ramsay, his employer . . .

'But you shouldn't forget that traditionally we are labourers and are one soul. Our hearts beat at one for the cause of the labourers. We are a suppressed lot. Aren't we? But our master is a bourgeois, going by the Marxian teachings. All his concessions are for his own sake and not for us.' Hibson once again revealed his dissatisfied and sulky mind.

'Our master's largesse is not for his own sake. He is a trader who had invested a fortune. Shouldn't he get back a reasonable return? Our contract with him is for salary and other perks only. But doesn't he give us more than that? Free drink is not in our contract. You can't ask for free drinks. Tell me, can you, as of right?' Mike asked.

'No. But isn't what he takes as profits, the fruits of our hard labour?' Hibson asked.

'Your argument is quite bizarre. Are you a labourer or investor? Tell me ?,' Rodrigues asked.

'Labourer,' Hibson replied.

'Tell me who is a labourer? What part he plays in production?' Mike asked.

'A labourer is a person who does work for another for wages,' Hibson replied.

'Then who is an investor?' Mike asked.

'An investor is a person who invests money and builds up an enterprise,' Hibson replied.

'Then do you find any difference in the roles of an investor and a labourer in production?' Rodrigues asked.

'Yes,' Hibson replied.

'What are they?' Mike asked.

'The investor invests money on land, machinery, building, and also working capital. And the labourer has only labour to contribute,' Hibson said.

'Do you know from where the money for the investments comes?' Rodrigues asked.

'Yes. Mostly from financial institutions,' Hibson replied. 'Now let me ask you a question. Would the financial

institutions give money free to the investor?' Mike asked. 'No. The principal and interest have to be paid within a

fixed period,' Hibson said.

'Now who is responsible for the repayments? Is it the labourer or the investor?' Mike asked.

'It's the investor and not the labourer,' Hibson replied. 'Then what's your role as a labourer in the production?'

Rodrigues asked.

'To give the labour and earn our wages in return,' Hibson replied.

'Now we hope our questions are an eye-opener to you. Then tell me who is entitled to the profits?' Mike asked.

'It's the investor,' Hibson replied.

'Then if the enterprise is running at a loss, whose risk is it to make the payments due to the financial institutions and the labourers?' Rodrigues asked.

'It's the investor's,' Hibson said.

'Then how can you say that our master is taking away the fruits of our hard labour? If anything, he is taking the fruits of his own hard labour by taking so many risks,' Mike said.

'If Mike is right, how can you belittle the concessions given to us by our master? Shouldn't you accept them gracefully? Now what you're doing is taking advantage of such concessions and you're thankless, all the same,' Rodrigues said.

'There's nothing worth saying of it. It's with every other *Abkaris* too. No employer would allow the employees to booze during duty time. Our master is no exception. So there is nothing special in his actions to reckon him as having some extra grace and compassion for the labourers,' Hibson protested.

'Then what about the facility of free drinks? Can you ignore it?' Mike countered.

'What makes you think every other distillery doesn't do it?' Hibson's talk showed his ingratitude as was his wont.

'You're always sulky. You don't deserve any largesse from anyone. You don't know how to accept such facilities gracefully and be thankful. You behave like a savage – uncivilised, uncultured, to say the least. It's impossible to put up with somebody who always grouses. You enjoy the concessions and have not a word of gratitude for it. What kind of a man are you? It's very cheap of you to behave in this fashion, you uncultured demon!' Rodrigues spoke very sternly, raising his eyebrows in a sudden spurt of anger.

Everyone had had too much of the 'fire water' and their vision was slowly becoming hazy.

Rodrigues's use of the words 'uncultured' and 'uncivilised' ignited Hibson too into losing his temper suddenly. He was out of his senses. He jumped to his feet staggeringly and started swaying like a tree in wind. Rodrigues, knowing he was targeted, struggled to his feet too. It was more of his tactics of defence. Resisting an attack sitting put a person in a disadvantageous position. A standing man could not be subdued very easily. Mike, getting a vague sense of an impending fisticuff, too was on his feet and moved towards Rodrigues and positioned behind him, ready to interfere if the situation got out of control. All were swaying on their feet. None was the better in stability.

'What did you say, you dirty gunk? If you have guts, call me once more.' Hibson threw the gauntlet which was taken up by Rodrigues. Even as they were having a wordy duel, Hibson suddenly planted a hit right in the face of Rodrigues. Rodrigues ducked and the hit got planted on the face of an unsuspecting Mike. He fell at the unexpected blow. Before he could get up, Hibson too lost his balance. As Rodrigues suddenly moved away from the line, Hibson was forced to lunge forward too much to the point of losing his balance, and he too fell flat. Soon they were fast asleep in each other's arms, in an irretrievably hugging posture. Rodrigues weaved his way home with unsure steps. The next morning when Rodrigues came for duty, Hibson and Mike were fast asleep, still in their same posture.

The management knowing about the petty squabbles and silly bickering of the drunken labourers too turned a blind eye, taking it as a blessing in disguise as the labourers were happier with the free drinks than their wages. So the management–labour relationship was peaceful. Ramsay always thought happily of his largesse as something that prevented so many labour unrests. As regards the free drinks to the labourers, he knew he could make good the loss by adding cheap additives to pure alcohol, which would make the stuff cheaper. And cheaper the liquor meant more profit to the *Abkari*. The more there are free supply, the happier the labourers would be. The more there are free supply, the more would be the need for spurious liquor to compensate the loss. He learnt this valuable lesson from his own experience.

'After all, how could we *Abkaris* make a reasonable profit after paying a humanely impossible huge amount fixed by the government every year as licence fees for selling liquor? When we struggle to make ends meet in such an adverse situation, the government shows no hesitation in branding us as bootleggers. These politicians who man the government and their cohorts whitewash themselves as moralists before the public when they call us bootleggers. They surreptitiously support the evil of bootlegging to sustain in the society by accepting illegal gratification without any compunctions and then they feign having not seen or having no knowledge of the unhealthy goings-on in the society. The revenue authorities who are to unearth such malpractices are the trusted lieutenants of these politicians, who too are the victims of venality, blissfully turning a blind eye to such malpractices. But in fact the government makes us bootleggers in our struggle to make ends meet,' Ramsay the owner of the distillery soliloquised.

Chapter 14

A month passed. One day, all the people who had visited the toddy shops in the area felt uncomfortable. They were sick. It was the beginning of the end of many – some in the hospital, some on their way to hospital, but more deaths were in the taverns themselves. The news of the death spread far and wide. Ambulance, fire force, and police were pressed into action. But nothing could prevent death. The death toll was on the increase. The police arrested Ramsay, the *Abkari*, and put him in jail. That particular day, after their usual drink binge at the distillery, Rodrigues went home. But Mike and Hibson had gone to a retail outlet to make themselves more merry by tasting the hooch. Both of them felt sick and they started spewing their guts out. After half an hour of struggle in this fashion, they fell unconscious and in that condition they passed away. Luckily, despite the pressure from Mike, Rodrigues opted to go home that day and thus had a narrow escape. Rodrigues firmly believed that the Goddess of Naga had saved him.

Now as one of the security personnels, Rodrigues's duty time was that of a night watchman. In fact, he opted for night duty. He was always with two of his new colleagues, Roger and King, who had replaced Mike and Hibson and who too had opted for night duty; their reason for that was to make them free during daytime for their drinking sessions. Maxwell was unhappy about this work arrangement. He feared his father would make his home a tavern by inviting his friends, which would spoil the family's privacy and disrupt his own studies. He thought it was a difficult proposition. He wanted to know about his mother's opinion.

'Mom, do you know Father has made a change in his work time?' Maxwell asked his mother.

'No. I'm hearing it from you,' Mildred said.

'It's going to be implemented from next week onwards,' Maxwell said.

'Is it so? From where have you got the information?' Mildred asked.

'I met Roger and King this morning. During our talk, they mentioned it casually,' Maxwell said.

'Oh! He is out to bring yet another headache for you,' Mildred said.

'What makes you think so?' Maxwell asked, without revealing his opinion about the change. He wanted to check if his mother's and his own reasons concurred.

'You cannot expect him to be in the tavern for the whole of the day. So to me it appears that he would bring the stuff home and celebrate by inviting his friends. And worse, it would affect your studies. Think of such a situation. Won't it disrupt the whole of our family life during day time?' Mildred asked.

'Yes. That's what I feel too. But something has to be done to reverse the duty change,' Maxwell said.

'Shall we meet Ramsay in private and explain things to him and make him change the duty time as it was before? Knowing the situation, he might oblige. He's known to be a kind man. That's what I feel,' Mildred said.

'Mom, your suggestion is good. But there are more chances of it not working. What I feel is that there is the possibility of his thinking of it in a different way,' Maxwell said.

'What makes you think so?' Mildred asked.

'He may be a good man. He may be obliging too. But when it comes to keeping his employees in good humour for his own business benefits, which would be his first priority, he may take a different stand, favouring his employees,' Maxwell said.

'In a way, what you said is correct too. Yes. He's a businessman. And his business thoughts are paramount to him or for that matter to any businessman. So we have to view him from that perspective. No shrewd businessman would ever spoil his business prospects by alienating his employees, ignoring their harmless demands like a change in their duty time just to favour someone who doesn't matter much to him,' Mildred said.

'Then how to get rid of this situation in a smooth way?' Mildred asked.

'I think we should not be hasty. We should wait and then a way would open before us. Sometimes the problem could be self-solving too in course of time.' Maxwell's thoughts were acceptable to Mildred too.

Everything was going fine for Rodrigues and his friends, Roger and King, when their boss accepted their request to change their duty time. They approached their boss with full of misgivings about the success of their mission. But the permission of their boss made them extremely happy. Then something happened to cut short their happiness. During the night duty they took turns at having some sleep while the others were awake. Such adjustments were their usual practice.

Chapter 15

One day, strange dreams started to appear in Rodrigues's sleep. It was how his nightmares began. In his dream, he saw snakes everywhere. It was as if so many snakes were haunting him. The snakes seemed to slither fast towards him and then suddenly disappear. Then new snakes appeared. They were billowy, undulating, swaying, and twisting in a fearsome manner. His friends heard Rodrigues speaking a strange language in his sleep. This was his initial symptom. Once, in his sleep, as usual, so many snakes appeared. There was a snake which seemed to be the cock of the walk. It had a halo around its head.

'Do you see snakes everywhere?' the snake with the nimbus asked Rodrigues.

'Yes,' Rodrigues replied.

'Do you know who are they?' the snake asked.

'I don't know. A snake yourself, it's for you to tell me,' Rodrigues answered, awestricken.

'Then take it from me, they are your ancestors,' the snake replied with an air of assurance.

'My ancestors were human beings. Weren't they? How come they are all snakes now?' Rodrigues asked in great disbelief, and surprise.

'It's symbolic,' the snake replied, smiling, venturing to make it clear.

'Symbolic?' Rodrigues asked, more confused.

'Yes, symbolic,' the snake replied.

'I don't understand what kind of symbolism is in play,' Rodrigues said.

'You may not know it perhaps,' the snake said.

'Then tell me what it is. It seems you get pleasure in confusing me,' Rodrigues said.

'I'm not confusing you. It's a great secret of a great universal truth, known only to those who govern the universe. And the underlings aren't supposed to know it. It's something called the theory of symbolism,' the snake said.

'Then how can you make it clear to me?' Rodrigues asked.

'To me, it's possible,' the snake replied.
'How can it be?' Rodrigues asked.

'I gave you the clue. If you had gone by it, you wouldn't have asked me the question,' the snake replied.

'Why can't you make it clear to me, instead of giving me a clue to rack my brain?'

'You have to rack your brain only when you're clueless. But here I gave you the clue. Then why should you rack your brain?' the snake asked.

'If one can't get it, going by the clue, one has to rack one's brain,' Rodrigues said.

'Then take it from me, I'm the snake goddess whom your ancestors worshipped and I'm knowledgeable,' the snake revealed.

At this point, Rodrigues saw the king snake reared up from its lying posture, with its hood spread with pride.

'Then tell me that universal secret,' Rodrigues said, awestricken.

'It's a kind of mutation of the souls caused by cosmic radiation. This happens when the souls are free, I mean in a disembodied state,' the snake replied.

'But why my ancestors are snake-like in looks?' Rodrigues asked.

'Here the theory of symbolism works. It says the soul, in its disembodied state, assumes the shape of the god or goddess they worshipped, when it was attached to the human body,' the snake replied.

'It's so funny. The souls of the worshippers assume the shape of the worshipped,' Rodrigues said.

'Human beings lack this information which is known to their souls only when they're free. We conduct research to find out more details. But the cause of the free souls taking the shapes of the god or goddess worshipped in their life is established beyond any doubt. Free souls mean after the souls have left the body.'

'I have one more doubt. You told me all these are secrets not to be made known to the human mortals. But now you have revealed it to me. Then isn't it against your rules of conduct?' Rodrigues asked.

'No. Firstly, you are in your sleep. People like you would reach a rare higher level in sleep. But not all could reach this higher level. People like you are a class apart, called clairvoyants,' the snake replied.

'Then what's special in people like me to be called clairvoyants?' Rodrigues asked.

'Clairvoyants have the power to see the dead and talk to them in their sleep. It's because their soul leaves the body when they reach the particular level in their sleep. Then they can communicate with the souls of the dead. And you're one such,' the snake replied.

'But how do you know this?' Rodrigues asked.

'It's very simple. Only when your soul reaches this condition, you can see and communicate with us. And before you wake up, your soul would be back in your body, losing its status of a free soul. Then you won't be able to recollect anything of your dreamy condition,' said the snake.

This knowledge brought sudden new illusions in Rodrigues's mind. From his motionless state of sleep, he started slithering on his bed like a snake. Then he woke up with a start and found himself lying on the floor, having rolled over the bed. But he had no idea as to what had happened to him in his sleep. When he woke up, he was fully normal. It was for the onlookers that his condition posed a problem. He vaguely saw his friends staring at him in shock and fear with blanched faces, not being able to understand what was happening to him in his sleep. His colleagues Roger and King didn't know what to do. They were in a quandary. They thought of grilling him, if he had any idea of what was happening to him in his sleep. But when questioned, Rodrigues had no idea.

'I think he has some problem attached to his sleep,' Roger told King.

'It's not something to be ignored. It's something that requires urgent attention,' King agreed too.

'I don't know what it is. It could be some mental problem, I suppose,' Roger opined.

'But how could it be? During day time, he is quite normal. The problem is attached to his sleep,' King asserted his view.

'That could be the reason he couldn't remember anything in his conscious state,' Roger too agreed with King.

'Who knows he wouldn't turn against us one day?' Roger expressed his apprehensions.

'Chances are there.' King too shared his apprehension with Roger. The thought put them in jitters.

'Oh, What was he doing the other night!' Roger exclaimed.

'Slithering, meandering like a boneless creature. How could a man move his body in a zigzag form, so long, non-stop. He glided, slid, and finally rolled over his bed on to the floor. What would have been the result if he had accidentally hit his head on the floor and died?' Roger blanched at the very thought.

'Then surely we would be framed as his murderers.' King too got a shock when he thought of it.

'It was as if he was going to die the next moment!' Roger said in utter fear.

'Then what was he jabbering?' King looked at Roger, confused.

'I couldn't follow a bit too,' Roger muttered.

'It was as if he was in a strange world, talking a strange language, unintelligible to human beings,' King recalled.

'Anyway, we cannot keep him here like that in the night,' Roger opined.

'We don't know if his condition is fatal or what will happen to him the next moment. So it's better for him to stay home in the night and take day duty,' King suggested.

So they decided upon his taking day duties and staying home in the night. They informed Maxwell and his mother about the situation.

'You're having some problem. We don't know what it is. Perhaps you need some rest in the night. And in your present condition, it's better for you to take up day duty. You require to be observed in the night, for which you need to be home,' Roger explained to him.

'Ugh, I don't want to be a prisoner,' Rodrigues expressed his sudden disgust at the suggestion.

'Who told you you're a prisoner? You come here in the morning and take up the day duty. The only thing is you have to be home during nights. You require to be observed,' King consoled him.

Rodrigues was silent. He was not much worried of his problem, but was hooked to the thought of his day time freedom from duty; that would give him enough time to be high.

The duty was changed. Rodrigues was home every night. Mildred and Maxwell kept watching him in the night. As for Rodrigues, not a dreamless night had passed. To Mildred and Maxwell, those were sleepless nights, observing him. Each night was different for Maxwell. Some days he was heard murmuring. Mildred and Maxwell listened. They stood over him, keeping their ears sharp. But only the voice was audible and the words unintelligible. On some nights, he was seen straining hard, making his body billowy, in a snake-like motion. Then it was usual for him to roll over the bed on to the floor. Next morning, he would be all right, getting ready to go to work. He had no idea of what had happened to him in the night. Mildred and Maxwell were in a fix.

Chapter 16

One day, Roger and King visited Rodrigues's house to ask after his health. He wasn't there. They had discussions with Mildred and Maxwell about his conditions.

'How is he now?' King asked.

'No better,' Maxwell replied, looking forlorn.

'How long can you all keep him here in this condition without medical attention?' King asked.

'As long as we can,' Maxwell replied, resigned to his fate.

'And then . . . ?' King asked.

'And then . . . err . . . I'm not sure . . .,' Maxwell replied vaguely.

'You can't stay awake for months on end, watching him. Don't you want to treat your father?' Roger cut in.

'I don't think of impossibilities. I'm more worried about my mother,' Maxwell replied.

'What's wrong with her? Isn't she all right?' King asked, surprised.

'Yes, but . . . my father makes problems when he is asked to consult a doctor. He tried to attack her a couple of days ago,' Maxwell replied, worried.

'What provoked him?' King asked, a bit surprised . . .

'Mother talked about consulting a doctor,' Maxwell sighed.

'And then . . . ?' King asked inquisitively.

'He bashed her. "You all are making me a prisoner. It's so disgusting. What am I suffering from? Tell me. You people have gone nuts",' Maxwell quoted his father as saying.

'How much I love my mother! She is a paradigm of patience against the vagaries of my father. But I cannot allow her to suffer. I can't bear it . . . my mother's sufferings, for no fault of hers,' Maxwell replied. His eyes were moist.

'Then what did you do when your father attacked your mother?' Roger asked sympathetically.

'I interfered. But he pushed me aside and warned me with his usual refrain that he will stop paying for my education. He told me to go out of his house, that he didn't want any extra in his house, that I'm old enough to look after myself. He called me a noxious parasite,' Maxwell said sadly.

'Then what did you do?' King asked.

'His harsh words silenced me. Presently, I can't finish my education to get a job without his help, to escape from this domestic melee,' Maxwell replied, apprehensive about his future, which worried him no end.

'What you did is absolutely correct. You played it safe. And take care, you have to keep him in good humour till you get a job,' King said, thinking over how to solve the problem that was getting more and more complicated . . .

'Then don't you worry. We take up the responsibility. We expect him to pay heed to our suggestions,' Roger said hopefully.

'The problem couldn't be organic,' King gave out his findings.

'It's psychological, that's what I feel.' Roger's reply showed that their thoughts were identical.

'There is a priest in Coorg who is known to have cured so many. We plan to take him there. But I feel it's as well not an easy task, going by his opposing stand,' Mildred replied with concern.

'I think I could find out someone. I know one who is a psychologist. I will contact him and fix an appointment,' Roger suggested.

'No, a psychologist won't do. His ways are counselling – endless talks through so many sittings, which takes time. Only through urgent medication, the symptoms could be arrested. So a psychiatrist is the right person. What do you say?' Roger asked, turning to Mildred.

He noticed a change in her face. She was apathetic. Maxwell knew the reason. He knew she believed in the saying: 'More things are brought about by prayers than the world dreams of.' So he came to his mother's rescue.

'Let's try the priest first. His problem might be due to his guilt. Installation of the snake shrine in our courtyard is anti-godly for a Christian, which act may have caused a conflicting impact on his mind that he had committed a sin. So the conflict could be done away with, through prayers. Then the priest is the best person,' Maxwell opined. His opinion was a calculated one to support his mother's. He wasn't that keen either way.

'If that's so, let us try the priest, and if he fails, we will consult a psychiatrist.'

'We are Rodrigues's well-meaning friends. But we shouldn't interfere in his family affairs too much. We should give preference to their opinion,' King told Roger.

'At present, we are leaving. You come to a decision. And you can always expect all our cooperation. If you can't convince your father, tell us, then we would make him agree. So don't you worry,' Roger assured.

It was a task for Maxwell and Mildred to get his consent to visit the priest. Despite all their efforts, Rodrigues refused to budge. He was all right in his conscious condition. So it was very difficult to convince him.

'Why must you take me to the priest or a doctor?' Rodrigues asked.

'You have some problems,' Maxwell replied.

'What kind of problem? You're creating problems for me,' Rodrigues said.

'It's in your sleep,' Maxwell replied.

'I don't sleep during day time. If I have a problem, it's only when I sleep in the night. So you don't have to worry. I wake up in the morning before all of you,' Rodrigues said.

'But your nightmares can't be ignored,' Maxwell said. 'So the problem is with you. You are unnecessarily watchful. You don't sleep in the night watching my nightmares,' Rodrigues said.

'Yes. We don't sleep in the night, watching you,' Maxwell replied.

'You're to bother if I don't get good sleep in the night. But I get good sleep. And you spend sleepless nights bothering about my nightmares. Then I advise you to go to sleep in the night and be natural in your routine. Your problem will be over. But it seems you're bent upon creating problems where there is none,' Rodrigues replied.

'It's not always for you to decide, if you have some problems or not. Others too are concerned, if there is something wrong with you.' Maxwell feigned concern, suppressing his callousness.

'If there's any problem with me, it's me who should realize it first before others can diagnose it. It's the case with every human being,' Rodrigues replied.

'But there are cases when the doctors diagnose some ailment, when the patient is totally unaware of it,' Maxwell said.

'Then you aren't a doctor,' Rodrigues said.

'Then you too aren't a doctor. That's why we want you to consult the priest who cures through prayers,' Maxwell suggested.

'You're not to take a decision for me. And I don't want to be a prisoner of the priest or a doctor,' Rodrigues repeated.

'You haven't understood what we say. We only want to take you to the priest for a consultation. Advising you to consult a doctor is not taking a decision on behalf of you. And it's for you to decide whether to take up the treatment or not after consultation. Hope you have understood the difference. You're unnecessarily jumping to conclusions, that's the problem,' Maxwell said.

'My conclusion is a well-thought out one,' Rodrigues asserted.

Then Maxwell informed Roger and King of the precarious situation. They volunteered to make Rodrigues agree to consult the priest or a doctor, using their good offices.

'Rodrigues, we too are of opinion that you should consult the priest, and if he fails we would approach a psychiatrist. There's no point in being adamant. Problems have to be solved. It's better if it's at the earliest. Now you should know yourself. You have some problems. And we want to solve it. And as your friends, we tell you to cooperate,' Roger asserted.

Soon the initial objections of Rodrigues wore off. He agreed to undergo treatment.

Chapter 17

One day, Rodrigues, Maxwell, and Mildred reached Coorg in the morning. The weather was chilly and they had to use winter gear to warm themselves. The bus went only up to Mokeri. From there, they had to walk about two miles. But that was not a problem for them in the refreshing cold. The route was a rough pathway. As they neared the clinic (about one mile to go further), darkness fell on them, as if there was an early sunset. As it was a forest area, the huge forest trees and the foliage blocked the sun rays. Then as they progressed, they saw a hazy-looking object, not so discernible to naked eyes. It could be a building or a building-like something else. As they approached, the haze grew and the building-like object looked like merging into the thick haze, and soon it disappeared from view. They were confused. The situation was enigmatic. Then as if from nowhere, a man came closer to Rodrigues from behind. For a few minutes, they walked abreast of each other, and making use of those moments, the stranger stared at Rodrigues as if to fix him in his mind and then walked past. Soon he disappeared from view. A streak of fear flashed across their minds. But the guy was a harmless tribes man back from the town of Mokeri. It was habitual for the tribes men to stare at those non-tribes men who made their presence in that area. The darkness grew more and more dense. Then they had to move very cautiously so as not to be off the narrow pathway and get lost in the dark wilderness. Finally, they were in front of a building.

'Could it be the one where the priest stays? It's called a clinic but looks like a fearsome den,' Maxwell thought. They didn't know someone had opened the door, come out, and stood in front of them. They never expected him to be so intimidatingly close to them in the darkness and yet another bout of fear gripped their minds. The man was the priest. Maxwell wondered how the priest had sensed their presence outside. They were directed into a small room, where a candle was burning.

'You have a booking today?' the priest asked.

'Yes,' Maxwell replied.

Then the priest searched in a register and asked, 'Rodrigues?'

'Yes,' replied Rodrigues.

The priest looked intently at Rodrigues and so did he. The priest's face seemed familiar to him. Then he thought the feeling of familiarity could as well be a casual coincidental similarity to another familiar face. But a past incident instantly flashed across Rodrigues's mind, which he always wanted to forget. Eventually, some disquieting thoughts haunted his mind. He was restless.

Soon Maxwell and Mildred were asked to wait in the foyer. Rodrigues was ushered into another room. A few minutes passed. Then Rodrigues was directed to a hall situated in the interior of the building. A door was open to him. There he experienced an intense smell. He saw about twenty people there, sitting in a trance. Rodrigues was offered a chair. He was asked to breathe in and breathe out twice. Soon he too lapsed into a trance . . . Mildred and Maxwell waited in the foyer. After an hour, he woke up and the treatment was over.

When they were about to part, the priest asked Rodrigues to stay back. He gave him a packet which contained his follow-up medicines. 'This is different. This is for chewing. It's different from the one you inhaled. This is a mild stuff. As you have finished your treatment, this would keep you in an elated condition. This is what we do with all the patients who take the treatment here,' the priest said.

'Father, I understand, all your advice is for my own well-being. I would be following your instructions strictly. Thank you, Father, and praise the Lord,' Rodrigues said quite benignly.

'May God bless you and your family,' the priest said.

Then the priest was seen giving some urgent instructions to one of his assistants, who looked like a thug with intimidating looks. He was seen nodding his head in agreement to the priest's instructions. And soon they parted. The priest left the scene soon to attend to the patients who were waiting.

Maxwell and Mildred walked with Rodrigues to the town. They walked along the forest path carefully so as not to go off the narrow pathway. As they were moving forward and had about a mile to reach the town of Mokeri, they noticed a man following them, looking intently at them. Their minds were filled with a strange fear. Soon they saw four men coming fast towards them. The man who was following them suddenly disappeared in the darkness, seeing the four men on the scene unexpectedly. Rodrigues, Mildred, and Maxwell heaved a sigh of relief. Now, the four men were unsuspecting tribes men returning to their huts after selling their forest wares in the town. Soon they reached the town of Mokeri, basked in the afternoon daylight. The town was humming with activities. Tourists were boarding the buses parked there. The hoteliers were busy like bees, catering to the needs of the tourists. A tourist bus was about to start for Kochi. They boarded it. Apart from the lunch break at Vythiri, it took them six hours in all, to finally reach Vypeen.

Chapter 18

Days wore off. Rodrigues seemed to have settled down in his routine life.

It was as if his day-time boozing had been shifted to night. Every night, he came fully drunk. His nightmares seemed to have been a story of the past. Everyone was happy. Everyone was all praise for Fr Lobo Perriera, the priest who ran the clinic to treat mental ailments at Coorg, where he was taken for treatment.

In that way, months passed. The medicine the priest gave him as a follow-up treatment was about to be over. Rodrigues observed the changes in him after using it. It was a shock to him when he realised he could not live on without it and that the stock with him was about to be over.

'How to get more of it unless I go over to Coorg again?' Rodrigues thought in utter confusion. And one day he had to go without the stuff, his stock having been exhausted. But soon the expected happened. He felt giddiness. His mouth was dry. He started yawning incessantly. He had muscle cramps. He was so uncomfortable. And Maxwell and Mildred were hapless onlookers to his discomfort.

'Give me some water. My throat is parched. I have muscle cramps,'. he groaned in extreme agony.

Suddenly, it struck Maxwell that fomenting with warm water might give him some relief. He ran for the hot water bag, filled it, and started fomenting him. He felt some relief.

Soon he lapsed into deep sleep. The next morning he was found missing. Roger and King were informed. Soon the police was alerted. Mildred was sad.

'Good riddance, now my mother is saved,' Maxwell thought.

Whatever pittance the family got from Rodrigues ceased once and for all. Their primary question was how to eke out a living, let alone funding the education of Maxwell. They were hard pressed.

'I must do something to make a living,' Mildred thought in her distress. She told this to Maxwell also. But he knew he was ill equipped for his dream job as he had to finish his course and exam and wait for the result and an appointment. He knew all these were not hurdles for him normally, but in the pressing need of the time they all posed inescapable problems for him.

'The only solution is I get a job,' Mildred told Maxwell, suppressing her helplessness and frustration in the situation.

'But what kind of a job? You aren't trained for any except your job as a homemaker, which doesn't bring you anything additional by way of income,' Maxwell said, looking forlorn.

Maxwell's poser 'what kind of a job?' put Mildred thinking, and she grew anxious.

'I must get a job somewhere,' she replied; her face showed she was undecided as to what kind of a job she could get.

Mildred felt the days were flying faster than before. 'Yes, the days are flying faster,' she told herself. It was the urgency in her mind to get a job sooner that reflected in her mind as if the days were flying faster than before.

'Mom, the fact you aren't a trained hand for any job stands in your way,' Maxwell pointed out.

'You mean my prospects are bleak?' Mildred asked, wallowing in a mood of self-pity.

'Yes. Presently, both of us are in similar situations. You aren't trained in any job to be fixed in one. I'm only half trained in a particular job. My situation makes me feel I'm trapped in my way of getting a job immediately. As far as our job prospects are concerned, we're in the same dilemma,' Maxwell said in a fix.

'But, Maxy, now we aren't to harp on impossibilities. It's of no use. It would only put the problem to sleep rather than solving it. Let us find ways. Let us find out vacancies.' Mildred feigned confidence, suppressing her anxiety.

'Yes, Mom, we have to arrive at a solution, an appropriate one at that. But the scope of an appropriate solution is still elusive.' Maxwell said thinking the possibility of an immediate solution was bleak.

'It's the question of our family's existence, and the problem is to get a job in a short time. And the decision should be an appropriate one. This situation makes the problem stupendous,' Mildred said, down in spirits.

'What I would suggest is it's better I stop my studies and go for a job. And that looks expedient, setting aside our hopes and goals of life. More important is the question of our existence. And presently it's the only way out.' Maxwell looked as if he had taken a daring decision.

'What do you mean?' Mildred asked, astonished. 'Yes, Mom, I mean what I said,' Maxwell said, but in his heart he was so oppressed.

'Don't be foolish.' Mildred was on the verge of tears. She felt shattered at the decision of her son.

'It's not foolishness. It's the inevitable that's going to happen. When there is no way out, one has to accept the inevitable.' Maxwell feigned to be courageous in making his decision. But his mind couldn't accept it. He felt his life was in ruins.

'I would rather take up the job of beggary and keep your studies going, at any cost if the situation so demands. I want you to take your degree in education and get employed. No question of going back.' Mildred looked unusually determined. But deep in her heart, she was in extreme agony and distress.

Both the mother and the son were presenting themselves different suppressing their real thoughts.

'Mom, I thought of the possibilities of how our plans would work without impairing my studies. But I strongly feel thinking of impossibilities is a wasteful exercise. Now my time is bad. But it doesn't mean opportunities are closed before me once for all. Our hopes rise from our difficulties. I'm in a difficult situation and so are you. But does it mean it's the end of our lives. Certainly not. Our hopes and dreams are like the phoenix that rises from its own ashes. A time will come when our hopes and dreams will rise above the adverse circumstances we are destined to face.' Maxwell looked decided. His eyes flashed determination. His eyes had the glow of resolution.

Mildred knew her son was capable of rising to the occasion, but he would take a drastic step. And this was her present worry. Mildred grew more and more anxious about the stand her son would take. She feared one fine morning Maxwell would declare before her, 'Mom, I no more want to continue my studies.' Then that would be the end of all. 'Then it would be hell for me. And I must prevent such a thing from happening at any cost,' Mildred thought apprehensively.

'I must get a job. That's the pressing need of the time,' Maxwell reiterated.

'But where?' Mildred asked.

'Anywhere. My preference is any place where I can get one,' Maxwell replied.

'But if it is a far-off place, won't you have to go away, leaving me alone?' Mildred asked with a troubled heart that gave her more worry.

'That question doesn't arise. How can I leave my mom alone and go away?' Maxwell replied, displaying his determination and concern for his mother.

His answer pleased Mildred as it revealed his concern for his mom. That was more than enough for Mildred. All through her life she had been starved for care and concern.

Suddenly, a thought occurred to her mind momentarily and her face brightened up. Maxwell noticed the change and looked at her expectantly.

'But, Maxy, if you think I'm not trained in any particular job, doesn't the situation, in a way, make my job prospects wider? In the sense, I can take up any job that doesn't require any special skill,' Mildred said rather hopefully.

'Yes, you're right. It's a good finding on your part. If you're a trained hand in any particular job, you would be trapped and have to be choosy as it's in my case. Then the prospects of a job for you would be confined to that particular kind of job in which you are trained. Many of the employers take training in a particular job as a disqualification if the job they are offered is a different one and doesn't require any previous training or experience. This is finding an excuse to reject the application for someone whom the employers favour,' Maxwell said.

He thought his mother's finding that she had a wider scope for a job than him was right. And a ray of hope burst in his mind.

The finding as well gave her thoughts a momentum. She suddenly turned hopeful. She visited many prospective employers, but in vain. The initial setbacks never deterred her. She was sure her job prospects were wide, going by the sudden revelation in her mind. Finally, her finding proved to be right. There was a vacancy in Petronio's office. Petronio, whose office was just a walking distance away from her house, preferred only raw hands for the job, who could be trained by her at her office the way she desired. So, as luck would have it, Mildred could find an easy appointment with Petronio, who always preferred locals to work for her.

Petronio was a social worker with an office attached to her house. She employed as many as twelve women, including Mildred. She worked in the field of empowerment of women. Weekly seminars were conducted in which so many local women took part. Mildred was given field work. Her job was to meet women, spread the message, the motto of empowerment of women, and recruit them into the organisation in which she worked. Those who were members of the organisation had to pay a fee for the running of the office and salary to the employees. It was an interesting line of employment for Mildred. The job gave her a boost. She felt she had changed into somebody else – a new one, A stranger to the old Mildred, more desirable, more wanted than a housewife in servility. She took decisions. The training she got made her capable of that. As a field worker, she took decisions for others too, which naturally gave a boost to her subdued ego. She felt her life was no more that of a wife following the dictates of her husband for the sake of domestic peace. She thought of her only son Maxwell who would have been in a better disposition had Rodrigues been a responsible father. So she wanted to gain more power for resisting her husband too whenever he insulted Maxwell as an extra in his house. She wanted to act both as father and mother to Maxwell. The salary was enough to make ends meet. In the changed situation, Maxwell decided to continue his studies.

Chapter 19

One day, Mildred and Maxwell were talking. He wanted to ask his mother the question which he had in his mind since his father had absconded. Maxwell's mind was in a kind of push–pull condition to ask or not to ask, which made him diffident initially. But later the force of his inquisitiveness pushed him to ask.

Mildred noticed her son was up to something. She sensed her son was readying himself to ask something momentous, which made her straighten her back to wait readily for hearing something different from the casual talk they would have.

'Mom, I would like to know what is life to you now in my father's absence?' Maxwell asked quietly, yet a little diffidently too. His love for his mother was so intense that he didn't want to either hurt or insult her by asking questions that raked up her gory past. This was the reason that put him in two minds whether to ask or not. He quite reasonably thought she must be happy as his absence marked the end of her sufferings. But his mother's sad disposition after her husband's disappearance was contrary to his expectations. All the while, Maxwell was keeping the question in his mind for the appropriate time to come.

'What makes you ask such a question?' Mildred asked a counter question.

'Now there's peace in our home. You go to work. You earn. Everything goes smoothly. I strongly feel we're in a better disposition in Father's absence. When my father was alive, he gave you hell. Not a day had passed without his bashing you. Life was hell and frustration for you and me then. That's what made me ask the question,' Maxwell said, having got rid of his initial reticence.

'I don't worry of frustration in the past or now. If your father is home, it's frustration for me. Is that what you say? But if he is away and doesn't come back, then too it's frustration for me. So his presence or absence doesn't make any difference to me. So what's wrong in thinking positively, taking the situation in the stride?' Mildred replied.

'If that's the line of your thinking, I have nothing to say. But one thing, when you were harassed, it wasn't something concerning you alone. It made me so unhappy too. And I had to be a hapless silent witness because of my father's warning to me. How could I be a silent witness when my mother was bashed by a drunkard who sorely happened to be my father?' Maxwell asked.

'His absence spares me from being harassed. It brings about domestic peace. But even with all that I'm not happy,' Mildred said.

But it took no time for Maxwell to sense the undertones of his mother's statement that she wanted her husband back with the family.

'But it's not of much importance to me on two counts. As you know, he wasn't keen in funding my education. Then he frequently warned me he would stop funding my education. If such a thing happens, to me isn't it as good as he is no more to me even if he's with our family? And am I in the same situation now by his absence? Mother, now you're paid, working for Petronio. I know the salary is enough to meet my educational needs also and I know you earn for me too. So I'm happy in the present situation,' Maxwell said.

'There's no question of stopping your education that way. As your mother, it's my bounden duty to help you out. What I earn is not the criterion. It's of course a way out for you from the deadlock caused by his absence. Then as I'm here and working, my earnings are for your education too. So you aren't to stop your studies on that score. Accepting this logic, your father's presence at home is one too many. Or to be precise, peace and happiness prevail in our home and also you can continue your education uninterrupted, in the absence of the pressure put on you by your father's frequent warning. But is it all?' Mildred asked.

'I know. And that's why my question to you ; which situation makes you happier – Father home or Father away?' Maxwell said.

'Your question is not a shallow one. I feel it has deep roots in the minds of both of us, so to say. We face the same situation with different impacts on our minds and we respond differently. I can sense discordance. Though our minds are linked with a strong bond of love, I feel there is no point in saying we are one and the same or our hearts beat at one and things like that,' Mildred opined . . .

'According to me, Father away, makes me happier,' Maxwell declared, shedding all his initial inhibitions.

Mildred was silent for some time.

'What you say is right for you. But his absence makes me sad too,' Mildred repeated.

Mildred's revelations made Maxwell's inferences true. And he ventured to ask many questions about her views.

'Why it makes you sad . . . Mom? Isn't he a drunkard out of his sense and a habitual wife basher? But you say his absence makes you sad. So you like to be bashed every day by him? I hear your loud cries almost every day, to which I have to be a silent witness. And do you mean I should take your loud cries as an expression of your happiness in his presence? Your talk in this fashion makes me feel so,' Maxwell said.

'No. But my love for our family gives me the courage to suffer for you – to suffer for our family, which consists of your father, you, and me. And I feel I'm bound to suffer for the well-being of our family, for the integrity of our family. It's a sacrifice that makes me happy. That's what I mean,' Mildred said.

'But, Mother, I beg to differ. Sacrifice for the family becomes real only when all its members make sacrifices for the common good of the family. But in your case you alone talk about sacrifice. You alone make sacrifice while the other members don't, who only take the fruits of your sacrifice. This situation makes you nothing but a sacrificial goat,' Maxwell said.

'I don't bother about the others of my family when I make a sacrifice for them. I'm right when I make a sacrifice for my son, for my husband, and for the common good of our family,' Mildred said.

'Mother, what do you say? You suffer for me? Why must you? And if that son doesn't want you to suffer for him?' Maxwell asked.

'That's why I used the word "right". There is no need for me to get my son's permission, to suffer or do sacrifice for him. It's a voluntary act out of love. Did Jesus Christ ask permission from anybody for his great sacrifice on the cross?

But still those for whom Jesus had sacrificed his life welcomed his act as the greatest sacrifice in the world,' Mildred replied.

'But, Mom, Jesus Christ died on the cross for the sins of the people. So do you mean you suffer for my sins? Then am I a sinner?'

'No, Max. We always say Jesus Christ died on the cross for the sins of mankind. What we are taught by the church is Adam and Eve sinned first and as their descendants we too are sinners – sinners by our very birth. This belief is the basis of this concept of Jesus Christ's great sacrifice on the cross. As a believer, I'm to believe this,' Mildred said.

Both Mildred and Maxwell felt that they had strayed away from their point of talk. So Maxwell came back to the question they were discussing. 'So by suffering at the hands of my father, you do a sacrifice for me and for the integrity of our family because of your love?' Maxwell asked.

'Yes. Wherever there is love, there is sacrifice. And the driving force behind any sacrifice is love, pure and simple,' Mildred repeated.

'So you don't mind suffering at the hands of my father, for the sake of me? For the sake of our family? For the sake of its integrity? That's what you mean? But what about the trouble created by Father when he is home?' Maxwell asked.

'If we like the presence of somebody, we must bear the burden of his presence too. That's what I feel,' Mildred replied.

'Your words "if we like the presence of somebody" are a hint that you still like the presence of Father. Is that what you mean?' Maxwell asked.

'Yes, you're right,' Mildred answered.

'And you still like to bear the burden of Father bashing you?' Maxwell asked.

'Father's absence makes me feel something is missing from our family, as if its integrity is lost,' Mildred replied.

'But doesn't his presence too make you feel something is missing – the domestic peace?' Maxwell asked.

'I told you if we like the presence of somebody, we must be ready to bear the burden too, caused by his presence,' Mildred said.

'So you mean even at the expense of our domestic peace?' Maxwell asked.

'We must be ready for that too, as I said earlier, because the family's integrity is more important than domestic peace,' Mildred replied.

The talk ended there.

Maxwell felt sorry for his mother. Her views of her wayward husband seemed to him quite bizarre. He thought his mother's views were not natural for him to follow. He couldn't appreciate it. But he had to put up with it.

Chapter 20

Everyone believed Rodrigues could be found in Coorg, in all probability. Mildred, Roger, and King were of the same opinion. Maxwell wasn't that keen. He thought it was the duty of the police to find him. But he could not ignore his mother's feelings. He thought he must honour it. So the lot fell on Maxwell to make a search in Coorg. Maxwell started for Coorg by a bus that plied from Kochi to Coorg. Reaching Mokeri, he searched the probable places where his father could be found, but in vain. Then after two days he returned to Kochi. The bus to Kochi started in time. From the very beginning of his return journey, the conductor of the bus started watching him. Soon the guy had a hunch that his face was familiar to him. He approached him.

'I think I have met you before,' the conductor said.

'I don't think so,' Maxwell replied indifferently, as he was worried about the loss of the days which he had set apart for his studies.

'I don't remember where we met, but I think I know you,' the conductor persisted.

'May be a mistaken identity,' Maxwell replied disinterestedly.

'No. I'm sure I met you somewhere.' The conductor persisted.

'Are you sure?' Maxwell asked, suppressing his irritation.

'Yes,' the conductor replied.

'Then tell me where was it and when?'

The conductor got slightly offended, thinking that the guy was a little bit discourteous to him as there was no similar attempt on his part to find out. He felt Maxwell was feigning. But the conductor was travelling down memory lane while he talked. Soon he could recollect when and where he met Maxwell.

'Before joining this tourist bus service, I had a stint as the assistant of a Hindu priest. I think I visited your house at Vypeen for the installation of a snake shrine at your premises,' the conductor replied, his doubts giving way to certainty.

The conductor's reply took away the listlessness from the mind of Maxwell.

'By the way, what's your good name?' Maxwell asked.

'I'm Franklin,' the conductor replied.

'You are a Christian!' Maxwell asked in surprise.

'Yes,' Franklin replied.

'Then how could you be the assistant of a Hindu priest?' Maxwell asked.

'It's a story. By the force of circumstances, I had to feign to be a Hindu for my livelihood. I then joined a Hindu monastery and underwent two years' training for priesthood. I was an assistant priest. Then I couldn't continue there as one, because the job was a namesake one. Often I had to go without any food. But no one cared. The attitude of the pontiffs in the monastery was sacrifice, which was expected of a trainee priest.

The full-fledged ones always had a windfall. They were paid by the believers when they were called for some consecration ceremonies. Each and every day, there would be such functions. And their income was regular and to their heart's content. But assistant priests were always an ignored lot. And we had to depend on the mercy of the senior priest. No one was to question the priest's ways. If anyone did, they would warn him that he would be sent to the monastery for yet another two years' training. This was hated by everyone because the trainees were forcibly subjected to do so many things unwillingly,' Franklin explained.

'I thought you were well paid,' Maxwell said,

'It depends. Everyone who had money would not be lavish in making the payments. It all depended upon the belief of the person: how deep was his belief in God and the religious rites, how easily the priest could succeed in winning over their mind, etc. Then there were some who were involved in illegal business and earned a fortune. They always had a fear that their acts were anti-godly. Then they believed they could get deliverance from their sins by giving huge donations to the churches, temples, and mosques. And I tell you all these are beliefs. Belief has multifarious facets. But truth has only one. We would be entertaining so many beliefs when it came to religion, God, soul, etc., but failing to find if there is truth in these beliefs,' the conductor said.

'Didn't you have your parents to look after you?' Maxwell asked.

'Yes, but they were poor. When I reached my teens, I left my home for a job,' the conductor replied.

'Before joining the monastery as an assistant priest, what were you doing?' Maxwell asked.

'It was the question of my livelihood even then,' the conductor said.

'When I came out into the world, a free world was open before me. My present and future looked bleak as my past. But the need for making a living made me take to beggary. Then I knew the best way to earn money was to touch the cord of people's religious sentiments. I bought the photographs of Jesus Christ, Lord Krishna, and that of Muhammad. I visited houses for alms, projecting the photo according to the religion of the house I visited. Before visiting a house, I would make secret enquiries as to the religion of the family I visited. My plan worked. My income got a boost,' the conductor said.

'But wasn't it a kind of fooling the people?' Maxwell asked.

'You can't call it fooling, when my goal is a noble one of making a living for myself,' the conductor replied.

'If the house I visited was that of a Muslim, I would very carefully hide the photograph of Lord Krishna and that of Jesus Christ and project the photograph of Muhammad. Islam teaches to give away part of one's earnings to the poor and the needy. And what I got on such occasions was nothing but a windfall. They called it *sakath*.'

'Then going by your version, it seems to me your's was harmless but lucrative business. Then why did you leave it?' Maxwell asked.

'It was a thriving business. I was happy and contended. Then I realised it was only one side of it. And my happiness didn't last long. I didn't have an eye to see the danger involved. When I was begging for alms at a Hindu family, the master of the house just went inside to get some money for me. I was chanting a Hindu religious hymn, projecting the photograph of Lord Krishna. Before he came out, a dog appeared before me. It was after my flesh. I ran into the house itself to escape. The dog attacked me. Frightened, my voice choked into a kind of yodel, which then tapered into a kind of loud whisper, though I was still shouting at the top of my voice. Hearing my choked wailing and the angry barking of the dog, the owner of the house came, darting out. I lost my balance and fell down. As the owner came out, he saw me bleeding and struggling to get on my feet. He caught hold of the dog and locked it up. I was so upset. In my agitated condition, I never noticed the photograph of the Muslim saint which I had kept hidden in my bag had come out too. All my technique of praising the Hindu God before them boomeranged. They knew I was a fraud. The house was near a temple. The temple functionaries too came dashing, hearing the commotion. Coming to know about the story from the owner of the house, they surrounded me. It was the sight of the photograph of a Muslim saint that accidentally came out which provoked them, thinking that I was wilfully fooling them. I could not wriggle out of the situation easily. They questioned me severely. They tied me to a stake and battered me. My confession to them made them more and more angry. I got what I genuinely deserved. Some bruises still last on my body. And they were marks that marked the end of my begging venture, once and for all. Even now I firmly believe I got what I genuinely deserved,' the conductor said.

'When did you leave your assistant priest's job?' Maxwell asked.

'It was yet another incident that made me leave the job. It was the last consecration ceremony I took part and then I quit,' Franklin said.

'Tell me how it happened,' Maxwell asked. 'Everything was ready for an installation ceremony at a house in Alleppey. The house belonged to one Ram Govind, who was an ardent Hindu. But he worked in Oman as a Muslim by the name Jabbar. It was a grand consecration ceremony which was attended by so many Hindu believers. The priest started blowing the *makidi*. Everyone was taking part with their eyes closed. This time a snake appeared from behind. It came nearer and nearer. But the priest was unaware of it. Then suddenly the priest jumped with a cry of pain and fear. Everyone rushed to him. In the commotion, the snake cleverly escaped. Some people saw a cobra slithering away fast. But none could do anything. They were engaged in taking the priest to the nearest hospital. A taxi rushed him to the hospital. And the doctors pronounced him as "brought dead". The post-mortem report showed the reason of death as snake poisoning. Then I left the job. I didn't go back to the monastery. I learnt a lesson that "a man can fool the people once, but not every time".'

'Then how come you got the conductor's job?' Maxwell asked.

'Initially, I was a cleaner boy of the bus, Krishna, owned by one Royappa from Dahana Hulley, which did trips between Dahana Hulley and Kochi. I was in search of yet another job. I couldn't wait for a job of my satisfaction. Then the conductor of the bus, one Keagen from Kochi, asked me if I could wash the bus, when it stayed at Kochi overnight. I was given Rs. 1,500 monthly. It was not enough, even for my bare necessaries. But still I accepted it. Then I thought of getting the washing cleaning works of more buses that had overnight stay at Kochi. Seeing the quality of my work, two more buses came my way. I did my job to their utmost satisfaction. After a month, I got two more buses that plied between Dahana Hulley and Tamil

Nadu via Kochi with an overnight stay at Kochi. The payments of the other buses too were the same as that of Krishna. So my monthly income rose to Rs. 7,500 a month. For a single boy, it was more than enough to make ends meet. And I was obliged to Keagen, who had opened a way of life for me. Two years passed like that. Then more boys came to do the work. Then my income diminished. At that time, Keagen got a job as the conductor of the Karnataka State Transport bus. He graciously recommended the owner of Krishna to appoint me in his vacancy as a conductor . The owner was much pleased with my cleaning work, and so he had no qualms in taking me on as the conductor of the bus. My salary was equal to what I received as a washer boy. So there was no problem. Now I enjoy this job and am happy,' Franklin concluded.

Chapter 21

The complaint lodged with the police that Rodrigues was missing wasn't fruitful, yet. One day, as Maxwell was about to go out, he heard the doorbell and he opened it. He was greeted by two policemen in uniform. Their imposing visage betrayed something serious. Maxwell ushered them in.

'Please be seated,' Maxwell told them politely, which they did.

'Is this the house of Rodrigues?' one of the policemen asked.

'Yes, sir. Is there any problem?' Maxwell asked, though he could infer the visit was in pursuance of his complaint to the police of his missing father. He could infer something untoward must have happened to him.

'You had lodged a complaint with us that your father was missing?' the policeman asked.

'Yes,' Maxwell replied.

'Is he back home now?' the policeman asked.
'He isn't,' Maxwell replied.

'That makes our information correct. He's no more. We were in search of him in pursuance of your complaint. Now, we have solid information that he was a drug addict and that he had gone visiting a man who was disguised as a priest in Coorg, dealing in drugs, since he was at large. Now we have busted the drug racket of the priest. A corpse was found in the shoot-out riddled with bullets. And we have reasons to believe that the corpse is that of your father. Your complaint brought us here to take you to Coorg for identification of the corpse. In all probability, it could be your father's,' the policeman said.

'How come?' Maxwell asked unfeelingly.

'No complaint has been received from anybody else of a missing person. So the odds are in favour of your father. But if you can't identify the body, then there's the possibility of the body to be sent to the grave, unclaimed,' the policeman said.

'How does the face look like? Any similarity to that of any criminal known to you?' Maxwell asked.

'It's decayed beyond recognition,' the policeman said.
'Couldn't you bring the body to Kochi, as you have

reasons to believe the corpse is that of my father?' Maxwell asked, ignorant of the legal formalities.

'No. If we're to bring the body to Kochi, there are certain formalities. First of all, we have to identify the body beyond any doubt that it is of someone from Kochi. Till then, it's the duty of the Karnataka police to take care of it. And if the body is unidentifiable, then it would be buried in Karnataka. So there is no point in bringing the corpse before confirmation. We want your cooperation for the identification formalities and we have to do it urgently,' the policeman said.

Hearing this, Maxwell went inside and told Mildred what the policeman had said. Mildred's face changed to an expression of surprise and concern. Soon she was struggling to hold back her tears. Seeing his mother in tears, Maxwell who was apathetic to the information so far felt sad. His eyes became moist. But he didn't like his changed mental condition to be noticed by his mother. So he began to think of his father's wayward ways for a change of mood, to get back to his apathetic mood.

'Mom, it's not yet time to worry. We only got a doubtful information, yet to be confirmed and there is still the possibility of the information becoming untrue on identification.' Maxwell's reasoning was a facade, only to console his mother. But internally he really wanted the information to be true.

Maxwell and Mildred soon made arrangements to go with the police. Then they started for Coorg. The ramshackled police jeep carrying them zoomed fast towards Coorg. The monotonous drone of the engine and the rattle of its rickety body were high enough to beat all the other sounds. The mother and son didn't talk much in the presence of the police. So they soon lapsed into their own reverie.

'If at all the corpse is identified as that of my father, I'm the least bothered. But I only have concern for my mother and her loss, as I love her. And if the corpse is that of someone else and my father comes back alive, then it would make my mother really a sacrificial goat for whom a lot more sufferings would be in wait. Then I would be destined to be a sad, helpless witness to such situations in future also. My hands are tied. I can't interfere and earn my father's wrath in my present dependent condition. Forgetting that he has no concern for his only son, that's me, I always have to keep him in good humour for the sake of my own education – for the sake of my own future. Who would ever ask his son to go out of his house and that the son was old enough to fend for himself? Who would ever tell his son he wouldn't fund his education? Who would ever call his son an extra in his house and tell him to get out? Yes, he has shown me what I am to him and what he is to me. Then shouldn't my own life be more significant to me? It's a blessing for me that my mom works. She earns and the whole money is spent on our family to make ends meet. So it's better for me he is dead. Going by my mother's long sufferings, the information about my father's death should have made her feel that it is good riddance. But she is sad. She weeps silently. She surprises me,' Maxwell thought ruefully.

It was as if both the mother and the son couldn't understand each other despite their long and close association. Their thoughts were different about the same situation?

"The vast reservoir of human mind has unexplored areas where father, mother, son, sister, wife relations have no entry. It is a secret recess in every human mind – totally exclusive. This secret recess is the hide- out of man's so privte interests and goals, that makes him a different individual, a different personality. And this individual is never in sight. And this individual is always a stranger even to his own near and dear ones. So, if someone says, I know my son, or my mother, or my wife, my brother, or sister or I know my husband, it doesn't mean such knowledge about that person is unmistakably thorough, exhaustive, comprehensive, and total, covering the in and out of that person.

The policemen were talking and laughing, but Mildred and Maxwell continued to be in a reverie. Mildred was closely watching Maxwell. She hoped her son would do well when he got a teacher's job which was his passion. But she felt her son's attitude in the situation was unusually indifferent. Maxwell thought his mother's attitude in that situation was unusual too.

'Do you know Rodrigues had been in touch with any person or persons in Coorg?' The police officer who was with them asked a probing question.

'We have no idea of his contacts there,' Maxwell replied.

'Who were all his friends in Kochi?' the police officer asked.

'He hadn't many, except two,' Maxwell answered.

'Who are they?' the police officer queried.

'Roger and King,' Maxwell replied.

'Are they working?' the police officer asked.

'They're his colleagues. They work in the same distillery as my father,' Maxwell answered.

'Are they in the habit of taking narcotic drugs?' the police officer asked.

'No. They take liquors only,' Maxwell replied.

'How can you be sure of it?' the police officer asked.

'I see them regularly. They go to work daily. And they are very much here. They don't leave the place like my father. Whenever I see them they are normal. They talk sense. All these make me think so,' Maxwell said.

'Then how come your father alone turned to drugs? Normally drug habit is something that is passed from friends to friends. But it's unbelievable that your father alone fell into the habits, while his friends remain away from it. So I need to question you, your mother, and your father's two friends. And you're to be present at our Kochi office, when we are back from Coorg.' The police officer sent a feeler to Maxwell.

Maxwell was disturbed because his mother had taken the initiative to take his father to the priest at Coorg to treat his occasional bouts of nightmares, thinking that the priest could cure mental disorders through prayers. A firm believer in God and prayers, it was Mildred who overruled the suggestion of Roger and King for a psychiatrist. Mildred blunted the edge of their scientific views, telling them, 'More things are wrought about by prayers than the world dreams of', which silenced them. But now, things had taken an unwelcome turn. Mildred was so upset, thinking about facing the interrogation by the police. In place of the clarity and courage showed by her at the time of her decision, she now looked vague and frozen. Maxwell was worried too about the condition of his mother.

By evening, they reached Coorg. They were taken to the mortuary of the government hospital. Maxwell and Mildred were shown the corpse, which was decayed beyond recognition. They couldn't identify it. The face and body were swollen and the skin was ruptured and blistered heavily, which gave no idea about Rodrigues's face. Then the police asked him to examine the corpse for any other proof. Maxwell remembered his father used to wear his wedding ring on his ring finger. He asked the mortuary man to turn the corpse so they could have a full view of its right and left arm fingers. He did as he was told. Maxwell saw a glint of some metal part on its left arm ring finger, deeply embedded in the gangrenous flesh. The mortuary man put some force on the corpse's left arm to make the ring more visible. This caused the decayed flesh of the ring finger to slip off fully, in bits and shreds, exposing the bone with a loose golden ring on it. The name 'Mildred' was inscribed on it. The police officer verified it for confirmation. This was proof beyond any doubt that the corpse was that of Rodrigues.

Then the mortuary man tried to turn the body once again to its original posture a little. But the corpse didn't budge. Shreds of gangrenous flesh again came off the decayed corpse, giving out an unbearable stink. It was a nauseating sight. But the experienced mortuary man could stand it. When the body was identified beyond doubt, the Karnataka police heaved a sigh of relief while the Kerala police were saddled with the responsibility of taking the body to Kerala after post-mortem. When such formalities were over, it was late in the night. So they stayed in the Karnataka Police Club. The next morning, they all started for Kerala.

Maxwell was cool and composed except for his worry of the situation in which his mother was. When Mildred could read what was inscribed on the ring, tears trickled down her eyes. Past incidents came rushing to her mind, of the time when Rodrigues, Mildred, and her sister Viola were members of their church choir. Mildred and Viola were its vocalists. Rodrigues was the violinist. She remembered her love for Rodrigues. Mildred's sister Viola too had a fascination for Rodrigues. But Rodrigues loved Mildred. So they got married later. Viola didn't opt for any other marriage. She took the job of a teacher and remained a spinster. Initially, Mildred felt she was lucky and was sorry for her sister. Later on, it occurred to her that Viola was luckier than she, as she escaped a life with a drunkard. Soon she thought "marital life was not one of roses. It was always one of sustenance and endurance and not one to break off at the drop of a hat".

They reached Kochi. The body was taken to Rodrigues's house. A priest was summoned immediately as the body could not be kept any longer before the burial. King and Roger were informed. After the prayers at the house, the body was taken to the church. And after a short prayer in the church, the body was taken to the cemetery. Soon the burial took place. The two colleagues of Rodrigues, Roger and King, were sad. They had lost their friend. Mildred wept silently. She had lost her husband. Maxwell watched everyone. The tears of his mother were unexplainable to him. He felt his mother's mood was unacceptable to him. He thought how could a lady accept a husband who was a wife basher, who led a loose life, who ignored his family. Then it dawned on him that no one could think for others, that his thoughts about his mother's attitude in the situation as unacceptable to him was foolish. But he wanted to get an explanation from his mother what exactly drove her into a doleful mood. Then he thought it was not the appropriate time to have a talk with his mother. So he decided to wait.

Maxwell's classes went on in full swing in his absence. He made up for the unattended classes. But he was generally disturbed on account of the problems created by his father. It affected his assignment works a lot. As the final year exam was in the offing, everyone was diligent. And so were the professors. Going by the first year grades, Maxwell had nothing to fear about the final year exam also. There was no question of making up for a subject in which he got poor marks. He was confident of getting a pass in the first division or perhaps a first rank was likely to come his way. He knew this but was silent. The changed ambience at home changed Maxwell too. He wasn't the usual introvert in college. He felt like a bird out of the cage. His father's absence from home and his mother's earnings gave him confidence. One day Rodrigues's friends, Roger and King, visited his house. They were really worried how the family was pulling on after Rodrigues's death.

Mildred's job wiped out the major question of how to make ends meet. But still Mildred thought that whatever her husband brought home after spending on liquors would have been an additional financial help for the family. The thought made her nostalgic. The thought showed she still maintained her affinity to Rodrigues. She still longed for Rodrigues's presence at home though it was not to be . . .

Chapter 22

Weeks rolled off. Then Maxwell received a summons from the police station, asking him and Mildred to be present for interrogation the next day. King and Roger too got similar summons. They all reached the police station not a moment too soon. Roger was called to a distant room for interrogation lest his version be heard by others. Contradictions help the progress of investigations. That's why they were questioned separately. Then only the depositions would be realistic.

'Where do you stay?' the police officer asked.

'Vypeen,' Roger replied.

'How long have you been there?' the police officer asked.

'About five years,' Roger replied.

'What sort of a man was Rodrigues to you?' the police officer further asked.

'He had been nice to me,' Roger replied.

'What sort of a man is King to you?' the police officer continued.

'He is nice too,' Roger said.

'Is he in the habit of taking drugs?' the police officer questioned.

'Never,' Roger replied.

'How're you sure of it?' the officer asked.

'We are neighbours and work in the same distillery. And we have our boozing sessions always together,' Roger said.

'It's unbelievable. He will take liquors in your presence alone is not reason to believe he will not take drugs,' the police officer said.

'In our case, we had taken a vow to that effect. It's to prevent our drinking habits from crossing reasonable limits,' Roger said.

'That's fine,' the police officer said. The statement very much impressed the officer.

'Wasn't Rodrigues a regular in your boozing company? As you worked together . . .,' the police officer asked.

'Yes,' Roger replied.

'Then how did he alone turn to drugs without your knowledge?' the police officer asked further.

Roger felt he was cornered. He wanted to save Mildred and Maxwell as he knew they were innocent but had been responsible for Rodrigues's condition. But he could not suppress facts which would be self-incriminating to him. He paused a second. Then he narrated how Rodrigues happened to be a victim of nightmares and how Mildred had taken the decision to take him to the priest, who she believed treated mental ailments through prayers.

'Was the nightmares an affliction from Rodrigues's childhood?' the police officer asked.

'No. It was a later one,' Roger replied.

'Can you cite the reason or circumstances that led to the nightmares?' the police officer asked.

'As far as I know, his nightmares started a few months after the installation of a snake shrine in his courtyard", Roger said.

"What are the symptoms, you could notice?",The police officer.

"It appears in his sleep. He is seen slithering, meandering, in a zig-zag motion and finally rolls over the bed on to the floor. Sometimes he is heard speaking a strange language which was unintelligible to others. Then he wakes up and he remembers nothing as to what has happened to him in his sleep. Then he is normal. And nothing prevents him from his routine life and for that matter, going to work", Rogger replied.

'Ah! It's a clear case that needed psychological treatment,' the police officer said.

'But his wife, Mildred, a staunch believer in God and prayers believed that the priest at Coorg could cure such ailments through prayers and took Rodrigues to him. This was what had actually happened,' Roger said.

Then King was called. He too answered the questions the same way as Roger. As there were no contradictions in their answers, the police believed their depositions. So they were allowed to go. Then Maxwell was called.

'You're Rodrigues's son?' the police officer asked.

'Yes,' Maxwell replied.

'Do you have brothers and sisters?' the police officer asked.

'No. I'm his only issue', Maxwell replied.

'What're you doing?' the police officer asked.

'I'm studying for Bachelor's Degree in Education,' Maxwell answered.

'We want you to answer only one question. What made you select the priest for Rodrigues's treatment?' The police officer was testing if the reason for selecting the priest for cure as related by Roger and King confirmed that of Maxwell's.

'We thought the priest cured through prayers. So we opted for him when my father's friends suggested a psychiatrist or psychologist for him,' Maxwell said.

The interrogations ended. The police didn't question Mildred as they thought there was no need for it. But the officer called Maxwell and Mildred together.

'Both of you have involvement in the drug dealings. You're going to be framed as accomplices,' the police officer announced.

'We are innocent. We thought of a cure through prayers. We thought the priest was genuine, as he was made out to be. We had never known him before. Never seen him before. We didn't know who he actually was. Or what was he really doing in his clinic at Coorg. So please don't find fault with us. We're innocent. Please believe us. We never had any intention to be in the drug business. Though my father was a drunkard, he was never in the habit of taking drugs before,' Maxwell and Mildred pleaded.

'In serious cases like drug business, the element of intention is never taken into consideration. Even innocent people could be framed as culprits. An innocent involvement is enough. Knowledge is immaterial. There are as many as twelve similar cases pending before the court. And it's easy for us to conduct such cases, because we don't have to rack our brain to prove the knowledge or intention of the accused. It's enough if we prove his involvement of any kind. So you can't escape on that score,' the police officer said.

'Now you can go. You should not leave the jurisdiction of this police station without my permission,' the police officer affirmed. His face had an imposing look when he said this.

Maxwell and Mildred looked submissive, when the police officer said that. They left the police station with a heavy heart. They had walked a few yards when a policeman came rushing to them.

'I know you're sad and frustrated. We all know you're innocent. But in serious crimes like drug trafficking, or drug peddling, knowledge or intention is immaterial. Even an innocent involvement is enough. This is the law. We're helpless. What my officer said is absolutely correct . . .

But . . .' The policeman stopped halfway, smiling.
Maxwell was confused.

'Tell me what're you up to. We were told of the consequences by your officer and he had told us how our future conduct should be in unmistakable terms. Then I don't understand why you are following us. Why did you stop us and talk in this fashion?' Maxwell asked.

'As you know, law is for law's sake. It has no human touch. But you should not forget, the policemen are human beings in uniform. We can make or break you, if we so wish,' the policeman spoke.

'So you're here to break us?' Maxwell asked .

'I like your sense of humour,' the policeman laughed. Maxwell and Mildred didn't feel like laughing. Then he continued . . .

'But I have come to talk something serious,' the policeman said.

'I think what you are going to tell us cannot be more serious than what we heard from your officer,' Maxwell replied.

'It seems you're offended by what our officer has told you. But I tell you, what he said is what the law says. You know our duty is to interpret and apply the law. But you know, he's a nice officer who can do wonders. He's knowledgeable. He's thorough with the narcotic and criminal laws and their procedure. But he is more thorough with the actual practice. He could find holes and loopholes in the law. People gratify him and he helps them out in return. But for him many would have been cooling their heels behind the bars now. What he does is a kind of wonder,' the policeman said.

'Is he a magician?' Maxwell asked, slightly irritated.

'No. He turns things topsy-turvy within moments.

He makes an accused of this moment, innocent the next moment. He can make an unsuspecting innocent of today an accused overnight, when a case passes through his deft hands. These show his range. Yes, as you said, he is a magician: a magician of sorts. He's a magician who makes fantasies real in no time with a magical movement of his deft hands. People like you can only fantasise about escaping from being framed in such cases. But he makes such fantasies a reality. But he's a man of high ethics. So he never makes an innocent an accused even though he could. He makes the heartless law one of heart,' the policeman continued.

'How can he?' Maxwell asked.

'It's only the law is heartless. But the person behind to execute it is a man of heart. He can make the law dance to the tunes and rhythm of his heart,' the policeman replied.

'But isn't law rigid?' Maxwell asked.

'Law is rigid. But we make it flexible, when it passes through our deft hands,' the police man replied.

'How come?' Maxwell asked.

'Because we stand for the people,' the policeman said.

'Don't you have a responsibility to the society to book the culprits?' Maxwell asked.

'Society is a collection of individuals. The society has no stand, apart from the individuals forming it. So by serving the individuals, we serve the society. Hope you got the clue,' the policeman grinned.

'Clue? What's it?' Maxwell asked.

'I'm suggesting a way out for you, I mean suggesting to you how to get out of the problem and be happy,' the policeman said.

'So you mean it's a trap we are in now? Who sets the trap? And what's his interest in trapping innocent people like us?' Maxwell asked.

'Normally, a trap is set up with bad intentions. But ours is with good intentions,' the policeman said.

'You're talking about something new to me. Trap with good intentions!' Maxwell said.

'Yes,' the policeman replied.

'What you say is confusing,' Maxwell said. 'Experience is the good teacher. Our long experience taught us how to be experts in discerning who all are to be framed and who all aren't in a case. To us, the dividing line between the guilty and the innocent is very thin. I say this because it's evidence and not truth that brings the guilty and the innocent nearer. In such circumstances, ours is a very noble goal to save the innocent from being framed at all. If we're heartless, we could allow the law to take its course. But we wish no innocent should be framed. So we are on our task of saving the innocents. And for that matter, sometimes we may have to spare an accused. And in your case, to save you and your mother, we promise to spare your father too.

Sparing you and your mother and implicating your father at the same time is dangerous. If your father is made an accused, there's a possibility of your role too coming out in the evidence stage of the case. It's a double-edged situation. When your father's role comes out, then the court would find the role of you two in the case. Then the court would find fault with us for not including all the accused in the suit. To avoid this situation, your father too is to be removed from the list of the accused. You know the watchword of justice is: "An innocent should not be punished, even if it causes the escape of a thousand guilty". Our law is noble. It gives out the noble message of equity. It gives out the lofty message of fairness. It gives the message that justice should be tempered with mercy. And then going by the maxim, isn't our task noble, even if we set free a criminal to save innocent people like you and your mother?' the policeman asked.

'But, sir, my father is no more and no case will stand against a dead person. So wouldn't the question of framing us in the case too become infructuous?' Maxwell asked.

'Removing someone dead from the list of the accused is a different procedure. When we file a charge, we have to include the dead person too in the list with an appendage that he is no more. This situation doesn't call for the case to be written off. Even then his activities and dealings when he was alive would be investigated and reported to the court. When such an investigation is there, then the persons who are alive, with whom the deceased had dealings, would be exposed to scrutiny. In that case, you and your mother would have to be framed. So what we do is removing the offender from the list, from the very beginning, as if he's not in the picture at all. Then only we could save people like you and your mother. Do you get me?' the policeman explained.

'So you mean only the priest and his cohorts connected to his criminal activities would be framed? And my father, my mother, and I wouldn't be in the picture?' Maxwell clarified.

'Yes,' the policeman said.

'I hope you do all these things in your earnestness to see that justice is done to the innocent. It sounds a very good gesture on your part,' Maxwell said.

'No, sir. When we do this, we accept a reward from the beneficiaries. Frankly, the government is heartless when it calls such payments as illegal gratification. But to us, such a gratification is noble, pure, and natural,' the policeman said.

'Is it not disregarding the law?' Maxwell asked.

'No. It shows our great regard for the law,' the policeman replied.

'Is it not doing what you think is right?' Maxwell said. 'No. It's doing what the law thinks right: that an innocent shall not be punished, even if it causes the escape of a thousand criminals,' the policeman said.

'But isn't it a kind of defeating the very purpose of law?' Maxwell asked.

'Oh never! It's serving the very purpose of law,' the policeman replied.

'But yours is not a common man's view,' Maxwell pointed out.

'Mine is a policeman's view to save the innocent,' the policeman said.

'Shouldn't the common man's view and the policeman's view concur?'

'Who told you they don't concur?' the policeman asked. 'How come?' Maxwell countered.

'We the policemen want to save the common man from being framed in a court case. And the common man also wants that. So don't they concur? We are to decide who all are to be framed as the accused. If we know, as it's in your case, you're innocent, we can frame a case without implicating you. But the only thing is you must incur some expenses for what we do for you. And that's our policy. It's our goodwill,' the policeman said.

'Goodwill? It sounds so funny,' Maxwell said.

'Yes. It's so funny. Isn't it something funny when you are saved from being framed and we get something for our efforts?' the policeman replied.

'Isn't it something like mutual help?' Maxwell asked, his mood changed.

'Yes. It could as well be mutual help. It's the agreement of differently thinking minds: their marriage, fusion, identity, or whatever you may call it. We save you and you pay us,' the policeman said.

'Then what's your expectation?' Maxwell asked.

'It's fixed – Rs. 10,000, not a bean more and not a bean less. Then you will be saved from a big headache. Hearing what we expect, don't you feel it's good riddance, which itself is worth more than Rs. 10,000? And we are principled. We don't accept even if we are offered more. Our rate is fixed. Our officer is honest, decent, and not at all greedy. And he graciously gives you seven days for the payment,' the policeman said.

'Okay, I will make the payment, as desired by you,' Maxwell agreed. When he said this, he was unsure of the source from where he could raise the amount.

The policeman smiled graciously, shook hands with Maxwell, and soon they parted.

Maxwell was worried how to raise the money within such a short period. He looked around. The world looked wide. But the ways for the cash inflow looked narrow. Thinking of it, Maxwell and Mildred headed back home.

Chapter 23

Maxwell was in a reverie. He was in a fix as how to escape the trap. He felt he was being approached by two demons. His choice was to become prey to either of the demons. One was the need for the money demanded by the policeman. So long as he was a dependent on his parents, the question of his raising Rs. 10,000 was an impossibility. In his father's absence, his mother was burdened with the task of eking out a living and funding his education. And besides all these, raising Rs. 10,000 to gratify the police was beyond his or his mother's means. But it was a burden that had to be carried out, surely and immediately. He could not shun it or put it off for a future time. The only way to raise money, as far as Maxwell was concerned, was by his getting a job soon. But for that, he had to finish his education and then get an immediate job, which was an impossibility in such a short time. The police wouldn't wait for long. Why should they? It was their tactics of bringing the concerned to a pressing situation. And for that matter, the police couldn't put off charging a case indefinitely while they waited for the money to change hands. Any request to the police to pay it in instalments wouldn't work for the same reason. They were answerable for any delay in filing the case. If he failed to raise the money in a short while, the result was that he and his mother would land in the prison. The offence was a serious one, affecting the society. Maxwell could not afford to be in jail at a time when he was about to finish his education and seek a job. Then he thought of his father's wedding ring, which they had got back from the police by an order of the court.

'Pledging it is not of any use. It would be beyond our means to redeem the pledge. Then it would be as good as sold. Then Mother won't agree because of her sentimental attachment to it. So even my sounding it out to her would make her sad,' Maxwell mused.

Then he thought, 'How cunning and greedy are the police when they twist a law to favour the guilty by accepting bribe. Why find fault with the police? Weren't those who passed the laws cunning themselves, aiming at their own self-aggrandizement? The police could have exempted me and my mother from the case. They knew we are innocent. But going by the law we too are to be framed. It's a question of their choice. But why should they make a choice in favour of us and lose a fortune that way? They wouldn't let us go for a song. Cases like this are sure and safe for them to make money. They are not taking any risk. Letting someone go when he is to be included as an accused, due to his part in the offence, is risky. But they would set him free for money. But any time they run the risk of the malpractice being unearthed later on. So they too should get something for the risk they undertake.'

Mildred was walking by his side all the while. She didn't say anything. She too seemed to have fallen in a kind of reverie. Though none of them spoke, their thoughts were the same – how to get rid of the trap. The police wouldn't let them go unless they were paid. Then how could they raise the money to pay the police?

The thought of saddling his mother with an impossible task made his heart sink to the bottom. He was cheerless, in low spirits. A word of sympathy couldn't be expected of the police to come down in the deal. They could never ever be so kind. They dealt with the guilty and the innocent alike.

Maxwell was drowning deeper and deeper in his reverie, with no let up. But all his thoughts were about the policemen and their wayward ways. 'Thinking of them would not solve my problem. All my ways are blocked. How to move forward towards a solution? Where to get the money which I'm to pay the police? Regarding the solution of the problem, I stand where I stood', Maxwell thought.

If his father had been alive and was around, the problem would have been doubled. He too would have been framed in the case as an accused, as he was a customer of the priest. In that case, not joining him as one of the accomplices in the case was more risky to the police, as he had a direct connection with the priest. In that case, the police would be taking a bigger risk and then they would surely up the ante. But luckily it was not to be. This thought brought calm to his mind. But soon the thought that he wasn't able to find out a source for the money brought him back to the same difficult situation. Time ticked away fast. And the ticker in his rib cage ticked faster too, finding no solution.

Maxwell thought of King and Roger. He felt extreme contrition when he remembered his mother had rejected their suggestion of consulting a psychologist or psychiatrist for the sake of her faith in the priest, which had brought about this kind of stalemate in their lives. He thought the need for Rs. 10,000 too was the fallout of that wrong decision.

'What to do, Mom?' Maxwell asked, feeling ashamed of discussing the problem with her . . . He thought, as a grown-up son, it was incumbent on him to find ways to raise the amount all by himself rather than taxing his mother who already earned a living for him too.

'I too was thinking of it,' Mildred replied with considerable chagrin.

'May I put forth a request to King and Roger?' he asked hesitantly.

'I don't think they could help us. What they too earn is scanty for their sustenance,' Mildred replied in a discouraging tone.

'Then we would have to approach some money lender. But then we would be forced to repay in time,' Maxwell said.

'Oh! They are shylocks. A deal with them would mean our life in the streets. They are dangerous people, having no heart for others,' Mildred replied.

'Then what to do?' Maxwell asked.

'We have to solve the problem. We have no time left. I think I will ask Petronio. She could be of some help,' Mildred said.

'You mean a loan?' Maxwell asked.

'No. I will ask a salary advance,' Mildred replied. 'There's no way open for raising the money. We need it within seven days. Mom, if you get an advance of your salary, then there would be a reduction in the monthly salary by way of repayment of the advance. Then how would you meet the expenses of our bare existence and that of my education, which we are struggling to meet even with your full salary?' Maxwell asked.

'What you said is right. But there should be a way out for us. We are short of money and the time within which we have to make the money is shorter. That's the problem. And I think too much of thinking over it will make us more and more confused and worried. And there should be an end, if there is a problem. I have decided to ask Petronio for a salary advance.

She might not oblige if it's a loan. But a salary advance may be acceptable to her.

'My meeting her is not with hope. I'm fully aware of the possibility of a negative result. Then there won't be any frustration even if I fail in my mission because I'm prepared for it also. Hopes bring frustration.' Mildred unwittingly revealed her view which was just opposite of Maxwell's.

'I think the best idea is to solicit the help of King and Roger. I have a hope they could help us out. They are the two persons who know us and our situation. If they have money to spare, they may allow us easy repayments,' Maxwell said.

'But you can expect from them a favour as their goodwill. As I'm working for Petronio, I can ask for a salary advance based on my work contract with them, but not so in the case of Roger and King. There's no work contract between them and you as I have with Petronio,' Mildred replied.

'But does your contract make for salary advances in cases of an emergency? I feel there won't be a provision to that effect. Normally, you wouldn't have thought of such a contingency in advance,' Maxwell said.

'You're right. But there is a relationship by virtue of a contract. So that would be a prompting factor. I go to her for work regularly and do my work to her fullest satisfaction. Sometimes she asks me to do some extra work for her, which I do for her for no extra. These factors make her trust me. These factors make her compassionate. Besides, she is in need of my service. So she has to keep me in good humour too.'

'But there's nothing wrong in making a try with Roger and King first. Our mission may come to fruition. You cannot say my attempt is bound to fail.' Maxwell's speech showed that he was still undecided.

'This is our wishful thinking yet to be realized. But in times of pressing need, we're prone to think in this fashion. But they may not come true. So don't be in high hopes. They too are not that well off as Petronio, who has an up and coming and promising business,' Mildred said.

'I know, Mom, but there's nothing wrong in chasing a hope when we are in difficulties, even if it may not come to fruition,' Maxwell replied.

'It's fine to be hopeful always. But we have no time to knock at everyone's door. Time is precious and we are in a deadlock that way. Weighing the probabilities in both these cases, we have a better chance with Petronio who runs a business than Roger and King who are salaried and have only limited income which *ipso facto* restrains them from sparing some money for others' needs. So why don't I meet Petronio first with whom we have a better chance? I tell you again a contractual relation would be more result oriented than goodwill, pure and simple. A salary advance is part performance of our contract. And there is no need for one to feel ashamed to ask. But a request on goodwill is not so. So let me try Petronio first.' Mildred had a point there, to which Maxwell had to agree.

Chapter 24

The spectral figure that Maxwell spotted at a distance in the poor visibility of the night, which seemed to have been moving in his direction, assuming several ghostly shapes before it finally took the shape of a hazy human; as it neared him was finally confirmed to be his own mother, Maxwell had been waiting for. And she was after carrying out her mission of meeting Petronio.

'How was it?' Maxwell asked.
'No chance,' Mildred replied.

'What was their reason?' Maxwell asked.

'"The present financial recession has brought down my business. The return from my investment is steadily going down. And for that matter, as one who works with me, aren't you too in the know of things?"' she quoted Petronio as saying.

'Now the only way open to us is to approach Roger and King. But, Mom, these are shadows in our lives beyond which I can envision bright sunlight,' Maxwell told a distraught Mildred.

The failure with Petronio brought some frustration in the mind of Mildred. But hearing Maxwell's view, soon she felt she still had reasons to be hopeful.

Chapter 25

Maxwell got dressed and was about to go out when he heard the doorbell. He opened it to see King and Roger at the doorstep. He invited them in.

'Please take your seats,' Maxwell said.
They sat down on two chairs.

'Oh, what a coincidence!' Maxwell exclaimed.
'Well, what makes you think so?' Roger asked.

'I was just going out to meet you, and lo! You're right on my doorstep. Now what brought you to your old friend's house?!' Maxwell exclaimed and laughed, forgetting for a moment his woes.

'We have come for a particular purpose. It's happy news for all of you,' Roger announced.

'Then what about you? Doesn't it make both of you happy too?' Maxwell asked jocularly.

'We too are very much happy, for the only reason that the news we're going to tell would make the family of our beloved friend Rodrigues happy,' Roger said.

Hearing this, the hearts of Mildred and Maxwell made a sudden leap of joy. It was a momentary escape from their sunken condition. But soon they were back to their overwhelming unhappy mental condition. It was the realization that their main problem of raising the money remained unsolved. This was so because going by the stalemate in which they were, they had no reason to be happy even for a moment. So their momentary elation suddenly gave way to the disturbing thought of how to raise the money in an impossibly short time. In this situation, Maxwell would have opened up the talk of their problem of money to them first. But the happy disposition in which Roger and King were in and the great vigour with which they introduced the purpose of their visiting Rodrigues's house were highly infectious. It was this reason that prevented Maxwell or Mildred from presenting their problem before them. But still they couldn't make out what the happiness of Roger and King was all about.

Maxwell and Mildred waited, looking at them inquiringly. They couldn't make out what Roger had meant by his words 'happy news that makes the family of our beloved friend Rodrigues happy too'. They looked eagerly at Roger to hear from him.

'We're soon to convey a message to you,' King said again.

This brought Mildred and Maxwell to the peak of their inquisitiveness.

'Please don't make us wait. You must have a heart to know how anxious we are. Your words have brought us to a state that we can't wait for it any longer. So, Roger, please!' Mildred beseeched.

'The managing director of the distillery has informed us that some salary and perks of Rodrigues are waiting to be paid. It amounts to a lakh in all. And Rodrigues has been removed from service. But as his legal heir, Maxwell is offered that job too,' Roger informed.

To Maxwell and Mildred, it was a pleasant surprise. Their joy knew no bounds. They couldn't believe their ears.

'Presently, we are hard up for money. And a job for me is the pressing need of the time. It's so surprising these have come my way, unbidden. And in my present situation, it goes without saying that I would accept them. But one thing, as I'm soon to appear for the exam how can I join duty?' Maxwell asked, a little frustrated. His need for money didn't allow him to say 'no' to the offer. But the need for the completion of his current course put him in a condition 'to be or not to be'. Then suddenly, an idea dawned on him.

'Can I take up the job part-time?' Maxwell asked.

'It has to be discussed with the managing director,' Roger said.

'He's a nice guy so long as we are nice to him too. No doubt. But let me tell you one more truth that if we're dishonest and insincere to him he will unmistakably show you the rude and vengeful side of his character.'

'What you said is absolutely correct. He's a good soul,' Maxwell added in agreement.

'Anyway, this is not the time for such a discussion. Let us meet him before he leaves the office,' Roger said.

So they all proceeded for the distillery. Mildred stayed back.

'The managing director would be able to sort out your problem,' King said.

Reaching the office, they saw the managing director in his office.

'Come in please,' the managing director called.

They all entered the office. They were asked to be seated. Then Maxwell opened up. He explained his problems, and asked the managing director if he could make the job a part-time one.

'Part-time job? So far I didn't give a thought to it. But I think I can arrange it that way for you,' the managing director said.

Maxwell had no difficulty in agreeing and signing the contract. And he was also given Rodrigues's balance of salary and perks to the tune of rupees one lakh. He thanked them all and walked home. When he reached home, Mildred and Maxwell were happy. He took Rs. 10,000 to pay the police and the balance amount was given to Mildred for her keeps. The next morning, he dashed to the police station. He was ushered to the officer. And soon the money changed hands, and in no time, Maxwell got their names removed from the array of the names of the accused along with his father's. Heaving a sigh of relief, he walked home.

Chapter 26

Reaching home, Maxwell experienced an unwonted ease. All the financial problems have been solved at one go unexpectedly.

'Some people bring happiness to their family by coming. But strangely, some people bring happiness by going. In this context, the second case is true for us. If my father were home now, we would have been deprived of the happiness of this occasion. And we would be destined to live on cash-strapped and our genuine needs un-served. I'm happy now. I'm happy on this occasion,' Maxwell thought. He told this to Mildred to get her opinion.

'I only feel we have surpassed one of our difficult situations in our life. But by your present elated disposition, I feel you think you have achieved everything in your life. But is it so?' Mildred asked.

'Mom, I can understand your mental condition. You had been suffering from father's wayward ways. You had been bashed by him every day for no fault of yours. Now your mind is a subdued one because of the adverse circumstances in your life. So when an occasion of joy comes, your unhappy experiences cover it up. And you cannot enjoy the sporadic moments of joy in your life. And your philosophy of life is pessimism, so to say. You have a tendency to believe life is full of miseries. Life is full of bad experience. Your past was one such. In the present also, you are haunted by the shadow of your unhappy past. It engulfs your present. So you can't find happiness in your present happy moments,' Maxwell said.

'But what I say is you should not be carried away by momentary happiness. I tell you, life is the sum total of countless moments. Viewing life from this point, the moments of happiness in your life are nothing but negligible. The experience of a whole life has to be taken into consideration to assess if it is a happy one or not. There is no point in unbridled excitement and exuberance at each and every moment of joy, because life is not those moments alone,' Mildred said.

'But, Mom, this kind of attitude makes me feel that one could enjoy life only when one reaches the last moments of one's life. Why can't you find joy in moments like this? Isn't it worthwhile to have a hearty laugh when we could raise the money to pay the police? How much we suffered thinking of how to raise the money. How much miseries we would have been facing if we hadn't been able to remove our names from the list of the accused? In fact, the police officer has done a big favour to us. Think, what would have been our fate if he was a man of principles, never to accept bribe? Wouldn't it have been unending miseries to us, having been framed as the accused for no fault of ours? If you think that way, wouldn't there be sufficient reason for us to rejoice, as we have escaped the sentence of a probable life imprisonment?' Maxwell asked.

'But I tell you this escape is not all. We have to go a long way before we leave this world. We don't know what the next moment would bring us,' Mildred replied.

'It's so funny. Do you mean that we're not to enjoy the present moment, not knowing what the next moment would bring us?,' Maxwell asked.

'I'm not concerned with the immediate present. Life's happiness is to be judged when it is considered in its entirety. So I'm not carried away by the joy the present moment has brought us,' Mildred replied.

'I think I don't agree with you on this point. You speak of experience and fail to enjoy your moments of achievements. It's not experience but achievements that make the life fruitful. Our pressing need for making the payment to the police put us in a dilemma. It was really an impossible challenge, considering our financial condition. It was a very bad experience in our life. We were pushed to raise the money within a very short period. Then we were able to tide over the problem. And we achieved our goal of raising the money. Then we can be said to have achieved something. And so many similar achievements make our life one of accomplishment. And life is not the sum total of so many bad experiences alone to the exclusion of so many good achievements. Achievements make our life one of fulfilment, one of accomplishment,' Maxwell said.

'But I don't get you all right. Please clarify,' Mildred said.

'You speak of experience: past, present, and future. Everyone born into this world passes through so many experiences. Passing through the experiences of life may teach a man many things. He learns lessons from experience. But they never make him an achiever, just because he passes through so many experiences in his life. Even if he is not an achiever, even if his life is not one of accomplishments, he is destined to pass through life's experiences, once he is born. But just because one is born into this world he need not be an achiever. Good experience brings us joy. Bad experience makes us sad. But achievements always make us happy and contented. Experience never has the glint and glitter of achievement. It calls for hard work for a goal and this makes achievements noble. I speak of such achievements. They need not be great achievements. Achievements are not determined by their greatness. Sometimes an achievement may be a great one. Then the achiever receives wide acclaim from the people. He becomes known to the world. Lesser achievements do not make the achiever famous, but still he is an achiever. He may be an achiever in his own private goal in his life. The greatness of a person's achievements is not the lone factor that makes his life one of accomplishments. Even in our private life, we become achievers. Even then it gives rise to a cause to rejoice. And I'm telling you about such situations. The fact we are able to raise the money for payment to the police in time is an achievement on our part. So we must rejoice. That's what I'm telling you,' Maxwell explained. The talk ended there.

Chapter 27

Mildred's thoughts flew back to the day when she had decided to take Rodrigues to the priest for treatment. She thought it was an utter foolish act on her part to take her husband to the priest. But she preferred the priest, thinking that it was prayers that cured the patients. And then it was her firm belief in prayers that actually misguided her, for the worse.

It is good to have faith, but it's bad to have implicit faith. Implicit faith rules out the possibilities of a reasonable inquiry into the truth. We believe in something. We repose full faith in it. Then to the believer the thing in which he reposes his faith turns out to be an unquestionable truth, an obsession and all that. And the outcome is the believer has to repent when the belief is disproved. The same thing had happened regarding Rodrigues's treatment. Instead of getting cured, he became a drug addict too. It was like jumping from fire to frying pan.

'Rodrigues's condition worsened after his treatment at the priest's. Then whose fault is it?' she asked herself. For the first time in her life, Mildred came out of the thin egg shell of her superstitions and looked around the world. For the first time in her life, she realized the world was full of superstitious beliefs. Sorcerers and black magic men thrived on the people's superstitious beliefs. People rushed to such tricksters, innocently believing their ailments could be cured at any cost and they would be made to pay through their nose before they realized their fatal folly.

'Roger and King proved to be well-meaning friends really, when they suggested a psychologist or psychiatrist. Maxwell simply supported my view of preferring the priest. He didn't have any opinion of his own regarding the treatment. But he was keen on supporting my opinion. His was not a studied opinion. The advantages of taking up the treatment with the priest or the advantages of going in for a psychologist or psychiatrist were never his concern. In fact, to be more precise, his view was neither in support of the priest nor in support of a psychologist or psychiatrist. At the time of making the decision, his mind was never in a mood to take sides, analysing the pros and cons and the advantages and disadvantages of taking up either mode. He was driven only by the thought of supporting me. Whatever be my view, it was his too. If I decided not to take his father anywhere for any treatment, his decision too would be the same. The fact that Roger and King didn't press their differing opinion was not their fault. Why should they? The question of taking my husband to treatment is a question of our family. So Roger and King had limitations. They played their part well by making the suggestion. But the decision was one to be taken by the members of the family. So they couldn't be found fault with. Then who is really responsible for the grave situation of Rodrigues? It's me and me alone,' Mildred thought sadly.

Chapter 28

One day, Roger and King paid a visit to Rodrigues's house. Their faces had a contented look. Maxwell and Mildred were there. They handed out a paper to Maxwell. It was his appointment order to join duty as part-time security in the distillery. He went through it. His duty schedule was very much acceptable – four hours in the evening, from 6 p.m. to 10 p.m. The order stated his duty on holidays was from 8 a.m. to 6 p.m. He was allowed to take full day leave for a week before the exam. And all the days of exam would be leave with pay. He thought his employer was a nice soul. He had allowed him to do his assignments during duty time. It was a longer leash for him alone. He was allowed time for preparations for the exam. As per the order, he was to join duty two days hence. After some time, Roger and King left.

Maxwell's face had a gleam. His mind asserted once again that there was substance in old adages. Once again he remembered the adage: 'Some people make you happy by coming while some people make you happy by going.' He felt those words were especially meant for him. When his father was with the family, their nights were nightmarish. Sometimes his father reached home after a nightly drunken brawl. His father's bullying of his mother was a regular affair under the influence of liquor. And he was a hapless witness to the scene. To him, those days were disgusting. He had to be patient for some more months. Now with the death of his father, he was an emancipated youth. His mother's nights were fearless ones. His father's salary arrears and perks stood him in good financial stead. There was peace at home. The arrears of salary and perks were enough to stand his educational expenses. Mother's earnings were enough to meet their living expenses. This change in Maxwell was radiant. He used to laugh and crack jokes with his friends. This was in contrast to his earlier nature of a withdrawn man. More friends came to him. His friends' circle widened. He then thought of yet another adage. 'You laugh and the world laughs with you. You weep and you weep alone.' All his pent-up capabilities started finding expression. He was turning into a different man. To him, his change was a process of self-discovery. Like a caged bird out of it, he fluttered around gleefully. He looked a man of initiative. He turned into an organiser. The spirit of social initiative dormant in him found expression during this period of transition. He wanted to change the whole social setup, though he knew he couldn't do it single-handedly. He found the entire social setup was in a befuddled state for evils to creep in so easily with none to prevent the situation from taking place. During the annual meeting of the members of the outgoing batch of his college, who were soon to be graduates in education, he shone like a Pole Star. He held the floor when he sang a beautiful song. He never knew there was a painter in him. All his paintings were aimed at social satire. His thoughts were those of an iconoclast. He proved he was a consummate artist. He donated one of his paintings to his college, which occupied an important place in the principal's office. The principal advised him to conduct an exhibition of his paintings. Maxwell found this advice a good idea. He decided to conduct an exhibition in the Town Hall near the Ernakulam North Railway overbridge. The principal inaugurated it. It was a three days' programme. All his paintings were sold for the price quoted on the tags.

'What more is needed to show you're a versatile genius?' the principal asked in his speech in the concluding function of the exhibition. Maxwell became the star of his college.

The exhibition brought him Rs. 1,00,000. It was like a windfall.

'A job and a teacher's one at that is my aim, which is certain to bring me a steady income. To settle down with a family, I must get my dream job of a teacher,' Maxwell thought.

He was certain of his plans. Exhibition of paintings could be done as a side business, as a way of some additional income. 'Moreover, it is my fond ambition to become a teacher. To me, it's not a profession. It's a way of life. There are so many things that make a teacher's job interesting to me. I won't like a teacher's job, if I don't like the ambience of the school where I'm posted,' Maxwell firmed up his mind regarding his future plans. Then he thought of getting a job as a teacher. He was sure he would get it. Going by his performance in the first year, he was sure to pass in the first division in the final year exam too.

Chapter 29

The day of Maxwell's joining the duty arrived. He reached the distillery and took charge exactly at 6 p.m. His employer was ready to brief him about his duties. Besides, he was so kind to tell him to take one or two books for his studies while he was on duty. 'As a security, you have responsibilities. You needn't walk around the factory like a watchdog. You have to attend nightly telephone calls till your duty is over.' Maxwell's duty time reduced Roger's and King's from 10 p.m. to 8 a.m. How to go ahead with the studies and job were Maxwell's initial apprehension. But one or two days of duty made him comfortable and relaxed. Besides, his employer was quite kind and keen that his duty should not affect his studies. Normally, an employer wouldn't like an employee's studies to interrupt his duty. In Maxwell's case, it was just the reverse. He found his job was a bonus to him. He got a lot of time to read during the duty time. As the exams were fast approaching, he was saddled with a lot of assignments. He virtually shifted his study to his duty room in the company. He could cover the portions fast. He felt he was reborn. He felt he was rejuvenated. All his plans of future were rekindled. His lethargic attitude towards his life was gone. He thought the uncertainty of his future was replaced with certainty. As regards his duty commitments, it was really aiding his assignment works. He had definite time for his duty. And he could devote this time more to his studies without any distraction. He felt his employer was a great man whose kindness made his life move as desired by him.

'But I like to be a teacher. And the present job is only a stopgap one for me. Of course, it's for the better. It makes the life of my mother and mine easy. It makes our life relaxed, and it makes our life problem free. This is the point from where our life really hurtles off at a speed of its own, with a momentum of its own, towards a goal of its own. We are happy. We are contented. We are now proud self dependants since the death of my father,' Maxwell thought.

Chapter 30

Maxwell had a talk at length with his mother when his father absconded from home without a word to any, about how she viewed her life with him when he was home and how she viewed life in his absence. It revealed to him her strange views about her life with her husband and her life in his absence. It was during those days when everyone entertained the hope that his father would come back. But now he wanted to make a deeper study of his mother's strange mind and her views of life, when she got the information that her husband was no more. Now with the death of her husband, he thought his mother was experiencing the two phases of her life – her life with her husband. Then she wasn't employed. Then his mother and he had to depend solely on his father's income. What he could spend for the needs of the family was what the balance he had in his hands, after lavishing his salary on liquors. The other phase was how she fared in the absence of her husband. Her life too had undergone a change from that of an unemployed lady to an employed one. She earned. On the death of his father, her son got the job of his father and he earned too.

Then which life she preferred? When his mother came home from work, he put this intriguing question across to her.

When she heard the question, her face became sullen. Maxwell noticed her eyes became moist. Her life under his father had made her a slave. It had taken away her power to respond. She was silent. But he still persisted.

'I don't like such questions,' Mildred replied.

'Why, Mom? I'm just asking you the good and bad of our life in father's presence and absence. Any person could make a comparison,' Maxwell said.

'Everyone's life is good. Everyone's life is bad too. It's an admixture of both. Life is not good alone. It's not bad alone. The presence or absence of a person is not what decides the happiness or unhappiness of a life. Once I told you of it. There isn't any guarantee for a man's life in this world. Then life doesn't depend on the existence or non-existence of a person. Man may die. It may be the end of that particular man's life, but life does not die. It has its origin in a remote point of the past and goes on and on unendingly. Some people say life finally merges into eternity. Its beginning is untraceable. Its end is untraceable too, because it merges into endless eternity. Those who are born into this world are like swimmers in a big river. When some call it a day, others carry on. The course of life never ends. Some of the swimmers drown, but swimming goes on and on.' Mildred was a little bit eloquent.

'But, Mom, you haven't understood my question. You aren't asked to take life in its entirety and that's why you talk in this way. What I want to know from you is about the immediate past and the present of our own life. It's not long since Father has passed away. We have been living with him for long. Now I invite you to compare both these situations: our life in his presence and our life in his absence,' Maxwell explained.

'Maxy, you don't understand what I say. That's what I feel. Life never depends on somebody. So there's no point in asking me to compare our life with and without your father,' Mildred said.

Maxwell wanted to get a reply. His mother's answer didn't satisfy him. So he wanted to put the question in a different way for her answer, the way desired by him.

'Do you love my father?' Maxwell asked.

'It was our love that made us live together as man and wife. It was our love that brought you into this world,' Mildred said.

'Then do you accept my father's wayward ways: his drinking habits, his bashing you, his making you suffer all through your life?' Maxwell asked.

'They're his ways of life. And marriage is not love alone but its acceptance, endurance, and sustenance as well. Acceptance and endurance lead to sustenance. Modern couples separate on flimsy grounds. Such things happen not because they don't love each other. But they lack acceptance and endurance needed for the sustenance of their marital life,' Mildred said.

'How's your present life?' Maxwell asked.

'It's calm,' Mildred said.

'Do you get bashed every night?' Maxwell asked.

'No,' Mildred said.

'Do you see your husband coming home fully lit up every day?' Maxell asked.

'No,' Mildred replied.

'Don't all these matters make you happy?' Maxwell asked.

'No, they don't,' Mildred replied.

'Why is it so to you?' Maxwell asked, wonderstruck.

'You can't generalize pleasures. You can't conclude what all are pleasures to you are pleasure to others too. To me, marital pleasure is when there is mutual acceptance, endurance, and sustenance. So the pleasure you envisage is not pleasure for me. There was a time when my sister and I had an infatuation for Rodrigues. Then we were in our teens. When Rodrigues loved me to the exclusion of my sister, who too loved him, I was happy. Then I thought I was lucky and my sister was unlucky. When Rodrigues proved to be a drunkard and irresponsible, I thought my sister was luckier than me because she could escape a life with him. It was a time when I was immature in my thoughts. I lacked sagacity and wisdom then. But in course of time, life taught me to think maturely and my mind taught me to be sagacious and all that. Then my view of marital life changed. My outlook changed too. Life with your father taught me acceptance. Life with your father taught me endurance and it taught me how to sustain our marital life,' Mildred said.

'So you're not happy in my father's absence? But then you can't ever expect that happiness in your life again, as he is no more,' Maxwell replied.

'But that also is acceptance and endurance that sustain my life in his absence. Now I can re-marry, if I so wish. But then my family life with your father would not be consummate as it lacks acceptance, endurance, and sustenance. And that's why the big idea of remarriage never occurred to me. It's with the same austerity with which I accepted, endured, and sustained my life with your father, I now accept, endure, and sustain my life without him,' Mildred said.

'Well, I don't get you,' Maxwell said.

'I believe accepting your father as what he was, by enduring his ways and that way sustaining my life with him, was what made my life consummate,' Mildred replied.

'But your life with him is already over and you still have a life ahead of you without him. At this point of your life, can you say your life is consummate, when you have completed only a part of it?' Maxwell asked.

'I have already told you it's the acceptance, endurance, and that way sustaining my life with or without your father is what makes my life consummate. It's not its duration,' Mildred replied.

'I don't get you, all right. Please come clear,' Maxwell said.

'You seem to take into consideration only one part of my life – the duration of my life with your father. Then you say my own life is not over. So I can't call my life a consummate one. Is that what you mean?' Mildred asked.

'Yes,' Maxwell replied.

'You can consider life piecemeal, like premarital, marital, and post-marital. But talking about life, it includes all these phases,' Mildred said. She continued. 'Though life is the sum total of premarital, marital, and post-marital stages, you can assess your performance in each stage. Here I use the word performance and not duration. It's not how short it was or how long it was. It's how you endured each phase, how you accepted each phase, how you sustained each phase, however short the duration may be. And the performance at each stage makes that particular stage of my life consummate. So I can surely say my life with or without your father is consummate for reasons I mentioned above.

And mind you, I talk about my own life with your father and not his with me,' Mildred said.

'Then how about my father's part of performance?' Maxwell asked.

Mildred felt she was in a tight corner. The force of circumstances made her admit that her husband's performance too had been consummate. Maxwell couldn't digest her admission. He felt his mother was hiding something strange from him by a strange force of circumstances. He was confused. Her appreciation of his father appeared to him as something unnatural and ridiculous. Maxwell had seen his father's irresponsible behaviour towards his mother, towards his family. He thought of him to be different, when it came to his friends Roger or King or for that matter his earlier friends Mike and Hibson. He could assess his attitude towards his friends as fair and intimate. But he could assess him as a strange family man when it came to his own family. Maxwell was sure of his own assessment on this point as that of a reasonable man of ordinary prudence and understanding. He was unable to disbelieve his own mother when she said her life with his father was consummate. He remembered his own mother's admission on a previous occasion that she had suffered under her husband for the cause of her own son. He heard it right from her own mouth. But now Maxwell found her reasoning different.

'So you think yours was a perfect marital life?' Maxwell asked.

'Yes, to me it's so,' Mildred replied.

'It seems you now contradict yourself, going by your own earlier admission that you suffer for your son,' Maxwell said.

'I'm not contradicting what I said. But you haven't understood me properly. Now, as I have a son born of my marital relationship with your father, my endurance and sustenance of my marital life means not my life with your father alone, but with my son too. To me the word "suffer" is endurance. It could as well be tolerance. Hope you understood ..'

Maxwell had no more questions about that. So he put his questions in a different way.

'Mom, haven't you heard people talking about marital pleasure or marital bliss?' Maxwell asked.

'Yes,' Mildred replied.

'What does it mean?' Maxwell asked.

'I'm not to give a generalised interpretation, because the concept is individualistic. It's subjective. That's what I think,' Mildred said.

'You mean you can't standardise the concept as applicable to each and every one?' Maxwell asked.

'That's right,' Mildred said.

'Then tell me what's it according to you,' Maxwell asked. 'Let me repeat. It's through endurance and acceptance I find marital pleasures. You may call it marital bliss or anything like that. But these factors make me call my marital life with your father a consummate one, accepting the good and bad of it with equanimity,' Mildred replied.

'So you mean sufferings are pleasure and bliss for you?' Maxwell asked.

'It's not suffering alone. Whatever is in store for me in my marital life, whether it's sufferings, pleasures, or comforts, it is acceptable to me, and this state of my mind gives me pleasure. This state of mind makes my mind calm and settled,' Mildred replied.

'Living in the present, ignoring its pleasures and brooding over the past and its sufferings, is life according to you. It's better to say that such people still live in the past, ignoring the present,' Maxwell said.

'You make things blur. You twist things, making them unintelligible. I don't get what you mean by your aforementioned statement,' Mildred said.

'I'm not twisting things. Your mind is active about the past and passive about the present. You like to taste life's wilted buds of the past and callously cause the fresh ones of the present to wilt away. Your life's attitude should have been the other way round – enjoying the fresh buds and leaving out the past wilted ones. So long as you can't do this, your life has lost its meaning,' Maxwell replied.

'You're confusing things,' Mildred said.

'What I mean is to forget the past, live happily today, and prepare for your tomorrow,' Maxwell answered.

'Forgetting Rodrigues and you and remarrying another is not life to me. So your father's death never makes me happy, though it's to you,' Mildred said.

Maxwell would never have thought of any such reply from his mother. He was surprised. His mother's attitude towards life appeared to him very strange.

'Mom! How strange are you? Your philosophy of life is very special to you only. I never imagined you have such a strange face, accepting everything good or evil as part of the stride. There was a man who created turbulence in your life. You suffered him. Then you got a golden chance to live happily ever after when you got rid of him. But you don't find any pleasure in accepting and enjoying the opportunity. Your austerity in facing life with equanimity is strange. The way in which you hope to sustain your life is stranger. Your love towards a man who gave you only hell, when he was with you, is the strangest, to say the least. When Father was alive, he only gave you miseries. He treated you as a lifeless chattel and not as a human being with flesh, bones, blood, emotions, and sentiments. He never loved you as a wife. He never loved you as the mother of his son, that's me. And for that matter, I too hadn't any love and affection from him. He had no interest in my future. True, he had funded my education. But even that gesture from him was precarious. He was inclined to stop funding my education any moment. And I had to keep him in good humour. My future depended on my success in keeping him in good humour. And I feel his death is certainly an escape for me from his clutches. Certainly a great relief!' Maxwell said.

Chapter 31

After absconding from Vypeen, Rodrigues secretly reached the priest's clinic in Coorg once again. After the first day's treatment, he decided to continue for six more days. He rented a room in a lodge. The room was modest. The rent was Rs. 40/- a day. The food was extra. As he was in hiding, he made arrangements to have food served in his room and seldom went out except for treatment. As his day's treatment time took an hour only, Rodrigues had plenty of free time.

One day as he casually came out of his room, he met a person who was staying in the room next to his. His name was Patrick. He too was there for treatment at the priest's clinic. As Rodrigues felt both of them were birds of the same feather, they soon became friendly and used to talk for long hours. One day Patrick asked, 'Where are you from?'

'I'm from Kochi,' Rodrigues said.

'I saw you at the priest's today,' Patrick replied. 'I saw you too,' Rodrigues said.

'Do you work for someone?' Patrick asked. 'Yes, I'm employed with an *Abkari.*'

'Then what's your rate?' Patrick asked, not knowing the meaning of the word *Abkari.*

'I'm an employee under a government licensee, selling liquor,' Rodrigues explained, knowing the guy couldn't catch the meaning of the word *Akbari.*

'Oh! I thought you're a quotation man,' Patrick said. Patrick's use of the word 'quotation man' gave Rodrigues an inkling that he was a professional killer. Going by the goings-on in modern society, he could infer the meaning correctly that such people were goons, out to kill people for others for a fees. They quoted their rates to their customers who wanted to settle a score, political or otherwise, who entrusted the work of killing or chopping the limbs of their adversaries for a full advance of their quote.

'Are you a quotation man?' Rodrigues asked directly. 'Yes,' Patrick said without any compunction or hesitation. And then he added, 'We're professionals and an inevitable part of the modern society.'

'Then your rates for killing?' Rodrigues asked a probing question, knowing such questions had never disturbed him in the least.

'Please, our ethics never allow us to use the word "killing" or "murder". We call it "causing total loss". For "causing total loss" our rate is Rs. 1,00,000. This is something like a wholesale business. So the charges are low,' Patrick said.

'Do you chop limbs?' Rodrigues asked.

'Please! Our ethics never allow us to call it chopping of limbs. We call it "depriving of limbs",' Patrick replied.

'Do you do "depriving of limbs" according to the specifics of your customers?' Rodrigues asked.

'Yes, we do. Our aim is the satisfaction of our customers,' Patrick replied.

'Is there any difference in the rates between the right and left limbs?' Rodrigues asked again.

'No. But we would advise our customers not to opt for limbs, but for causing total loss. This is economical,' Patrick replied.

He continued, 'We do the work of depriving one or both legs, sparing the hands, or we do the work of depriving of one or both hands, sparing the legs. And I tell you frankly, among the quotation companies, functioning under various names, our company by the name "The Disposers" is the most modern for our unmistakable accuracy. Our ways are unique. There is not even a single incident in which the men of our company have picked the wrong man. As you know, all other companies in this field have had at least one incident of finishing the wrong man. This is because our *modus operandi* is infallible,' Patrick explained proudly.

'Why are you taking treatment under the priest?' Rodrigues asked inquisitively.

'I told you. Now do you know why other quotation companies have the blemish of causing total loss of a man other than the one targeted?'

'Oh! It's a tragedy someone has to lose his life in consequences of the quotation company's men picking the wrong person,' Rodrigues said.

'This happens when the quotation people lack accuracy. This is because they take drugs and go out to execute their mission. And in their hazy, inebriated condition they don't have the accuracy to pinpoint the person to be disposed of and they bungle. This is a sorry state of affairs. But our company never allows this. If we have work to be carried out, we come here for treatment for seven days in advance. This has two purposes. One is, just like the body builders go to a health club to keep their bodies strong, we come here to make our minds strong and sharp. After the treatment we are calm, serene, and accurate. This should be the real condition of a mind that ventures to dispose. Then coming to the remuneration part, our charges are negotiable, pliable, viable, reasonable, and affordable,' Patrick spoke out his mind with pride, smiling in contentment.

'I think your business is a vast expanding one. But why aren't you caught by the police?' Rodrigues asked.

None of our company men have ever been caught. The reason is our *modus operandi* again. We aren't allowed to execute our job fully lit up as the men of other companies do. They aren't careful as our men. 'They are likely to leave some clue in their inebriated condition and get themselves caught by the police. But still they escape with impunity,' Patrick replied.

'How come?' Rodrigues asked.

'It's a known secret, and don't you know it too?' Patrick asked.

He paused and then continued, 'We're brought up by the politicians who are our self-styled caretakers, who are badly in need of our service in more ways than one. So they have to protect us at any cost. Sometimes they want to settle a score with their political adversaries for which they need our unreserved help. Then in times of elections they need a huge amount of money. And we cater to their monetary needs. No political party can survive an election unless they have a vast reserve of funds. And we fund them.'

'But how do they protect such men against the society and from the law of the land?' Rodrigues asked.

'In case any of the members of a quotation company is taken into police custody, soon he would be forcibly released from the police custody to the safety of a political party. Those politicians keeping such criminals in hiding will call a press conference and declare, "None of the criminals would be allowed to take the law unto his hands." The police officer who fails to file a case before the court in time will get a punishment transfer for dereliction of duty. But this is a gimmick, an eyewash, to fool the general public. The transfer will be to a place more convenient to the officer in every sense. In fact, his transfer is as good as a requested one for him as a reward for causing delay in filing the case in time to favour a caretaker politician. Then the police file a case in the court, which would be pending before the court endlessly, as the accused would be at large untraceably. Then a time would come when the police could no longer put off the arrest of the accused due to the mounting pressure from the public. And they would approach the political caretakers who protect the culprit and beg to give someone to be arrested in the place of the accused. Here comes the real play. The names of some bold persons, willing to play the accused but having no connections with the crime, would be supplied by these caretakers. During the trial, it's easy to produce strong evidence for the non-participation of such persons in the crime and the court has no other way but to set the accused free while the real guilty will be still at large,' Patrick said.

'So the politicians are your boss?' Rodrigues asked. 'No, in fact we're the boss. And the politicians are subservient to us. We are bold enough to carry out their criminal intentions and we fund their elections. It's we who sustain them,' Patrick replied.

'Are you attached to any of the governmental departments?' Rodrigues asked.

'No. But we would like to be attached to the human resources department,' Patrick said.

'How come? Isn't it a paradox?' Rodrigues said in surprise.

'There isn't any paradox. All those youngsters recruited into our organisation are resourceful humans,' Patrick replied.

'Then don't you know that someone has to lose his life by your criminal act?' Rodrigues said.

'One man's loss is another man's gain. It's nature's unwritten law,' Patrick opined nonchalantly.

'Don't you know the great saying that no man can take away the life of another, except God?' Rodrigues asked.

'We very much believe in the saying. If you had known the ways and the *modus operandi* of God, you wouldn't have asked the question,' Patrick said.

'Well, I don't get you properly,' Rodrigues replied. 'What I mean is that there's no homogeneity as for the mode of death of each man, according to God. People die in more ways than one,' Patrick said.

'That's right, and so what?' Rodrigues replied.

'God has preordained that one should die at such and such age, at such and such time, at such and such place, and due to such and such reasons. It's the wish of God. It's God's ways,' Patrick said.

'Yes, go ahead,' Rodrigues said.

'So if we cause total loss of someone, we are only carrying out the preordained wish of God. We believe that God has preordained that a particular victim would die at that moment, at that place, and at the hands of one or more of us. And we become God's tools in carrying out his wish. And we believe God is very much pleased with us. So we don't feel any guilt. The talk ended there.

Chapter 32

Before leaving for Kochi, he met the priest once again. His aim was to get the follow-up medicine for a longer time.

'I'm leaving for Kochi today,' Rodrigues said to the priest.

When Rodrigues informed that he was going to Kochi and paused, expecting the priest to give him the follow-up medicine, there was a pause, a silence between them. None of them spoke. But Rodrigues waited. The priest knew the reason why he waited. But he feigned ignorance.

'Father, it seems you have forgotten to give me something,' Rodrigues said at last, as if reminding him.

'Well, what is it?' the priest asked.

'Father, you forgot something it seems,' Rodrigues replied as if reminding him of something.

'I don't get you. Your talk makes me think I have forgotten something important . . .,' the priest said, again feigning.

'You forgot to give me the follow-up medicines,' Rodrigues said.

'Oh! Is it what you are waiting for? We're professionals. We never forget anything that is part of our professional work. But now you need not have to take the follow-up stuff. You could make do without it. You're allright now,' the priest assured him. He was sure of his future visits to him and that was what he really wanted. And he was happy.

'You no more need any follow-up medicine. I'm happy you have come back to me once again. Whenever you want my help, please feel free to come to me. May God bless you. And may God bless our relationship to last for days, months, and years to come,' the priest said happily.

'My aim to make my customers patients is a success. The follow-up medicine works to make my first-time patients addicts and confirms their return to me over and again,' the priest thought. He gloated over secretly that things were going the way as desired by him.

The next morning, Rodrigues was uncomfortable. His agony was on the increase. But he had no other alternative but to move to Kochi. He reached the bus terminal and boarded a bus parked there.

Taking a seat, he soon fell asleep. But he was watched by two men sitting in the back seat.

They sensed Rodrigues was in distress. They got up from their seats and sat on the seats next to Rodrigues's. The guys were experienced in the field they worked. They knew why Rodrigues was in agony and what he was suffering from. When they sat on the seats next to him, Rodrigues woke up. He felt some kind of a smell that was familiar to him, which gave him some relief from his extreme anguish and frequent yawning.

'I'm Kevin.' And referring to the other guy, he said, 'He's Ryan.'

'We're businessmen.' Kevin introduced themselves to Rodrigues.

'And you?' Kevin asked.

Rodrigues couldn't reply. He was preoccupied with his agony.

Turning to Ryan, as if he was assessing Rodrigues's condition, Kevin said in the broken jargon of their ilk, 'Our watch fruits. He looks very much in the field. Down and lowly in spirits. Looks a druggie for sure and famished. Looks meaningless. Novice. Wants backup. It's fantastic, if he goes by us.' Whenever they were in the field, Kevin and Ryan used the jargon of their ilk, as a protection from being overheard by others. Then he moved closer to Rodrigues and gave him something to chew. He felt comfortable in seconds and he started to talk.

'I'm Rodrigues from Vypeen,' Rodrigues replied, relieved of his agony and having been carried away by his friendly gesture.

'You're using a jumble of meaningless words. I don't follow you. Tell me what are you up to. I don't get you,' Rodrigues said.

'I'm sorry, it's our jargon. We can't help using it in public,' Kevin replied.

'What do you mean by the words, "our watch fruits", "very much in the field", "meaningless", "novice", "druggie", "famished", "backups", "it's fantastic if he goes by us"?' Rodrigues asked.

Kevin looked around to see if someone was watching and found none. He moved closer to Rodrigues. 'We're drug peddlers. We're always on the lookout for someone who takes drugs and sometimes our search finds fruits. We can sense drug addicts, at first sight. I sensed you're a beginner, not knowing the meaning of our jargon. You're listless because you're short of the stuff. You want my help? It takes you high. Usually we call it eats. Hope you understood what I meant.

We have to use our special jargon in public for security reasons,' Kevin hissed into Rodrigues's ears in better English. The smell of drugs passed into his lungs, and he felt some more relief from his discomfort.

'Now where do you stay?' Kevin asked. 'Some place, yet to find out,' Rodrigues said.

Kevin gave him some more of the stuff to chew. And he felt more warm and good, as if elated to a pleasant high from his sunken condition.

'Where do you stay?' Rodrigues asked Kevin.

'We live in the jungles of Mysore, among tigers,' Kevin replied.

In his elated condition, Rodrigues didn't appear to be bothered about his destination.

'Isn't it dangerous?' Rodrigues asked. 'We tame them. It's easy,' Kevin replied.

'But you can't tame all the ferocious animals in the jungle. So how can you be safe?' Rodrigues asked.

'It's not necessary. Quite a few would do,' Kevin replied. 'But how do you tame them when going near them itself

is so dangerous?' Rodrigues asked.

'We throw them the eats plain. They eat them. The next day at the same time, they come to the spot. Again we give them. The process is repeated at least for two days. Then the animals however ferocious they are become docile and start loving us,' Kevin said.

'Then what about the other ones who are not tamed?' Rodrigues asked.

'It's the nature of the tamed ones to be docile towards those who give them drugs. They won't bite the hands that drug them. And their drug habit formation would never allow them to leave the place where they get the eats, which give them a very rare, pleasant feeling. They never leave us but stay around keeping watch day and night and are so gentle towards us. But the ferociousness of the drugged ones doubles towards other animals and strangers. This is because that part of their brain that rouses reasonable apprehensions and fear in them like other animals is benumbed due to the effect of the drugs. So they are highly fearless and ferocious to face any enemy including strangers. But the un-drugged ones cannot hold on against the drugged ones. After a reasonable time, the fear in them would be roused naturally and they escape, accepting defeat. This too is a natural defence mechanism working in the un-drugged ones in situations when they sense defeat. So the un-drugged animals can't come anywhere near them. And what more is needed to make our lives in the jungle safe? It's as good as we live in a house in the jungle with all protections,' Kevin replied.

In his disturbed condition, Rodriguez couldn't pick up the right bus to Kochi. It was as if his mind was enveloped in a sudden haze, something like a blackout in which he lost his present whereabouts and destination. It was in that condition he boarded the wrong bus unawares, which took him directly to Mysore. But he never felt he was in a strange place. He was calm and comfortable, because Kevin and Ryan were very friendly and hospitable. Rodrigues wanted to hide his connection with the priest and his clinic at Coorg from Kevin and Ryan for reasons known only to him.

Rodrigues thought of his penniless condition, and a thought cropped up in his mind to go with Kevin to stay in the forest.

'But how can I ask him? He may not like it perhaps. Or his colleagues might feel odd in my presence,' Rodrigues thought.

Then suddenly, as if he had remembered something, Kevin looked at him.

'Have you decided where to stay tonight?' Kevin asked. 'Not yet,' Rodrigues replied.

'Oh! Going by your delay, I feel you're going to decide your tonight's stay only tomorrow,' Kevin laughed.

'Do you allow strangers to put up with you in your forest abode?' Rodrigues asked diffidently.

'Now I don't think you're a stranger. When I offered and you accepted the drugs, we became friends and members of the same ilk. I'm only happy to accommodate you,' Kevin said.

Rodrigues was happy and they proceeded to the forest where Kevin and Ryan stayed.

They travelled in a taxi jeep till the point where the motorable road ended. Then it was forest area. They had to walk through pitch dark. But Kevin and Ryan took care of Rodrigues as good navigators. After an hour's journey, they came to a place where there was a waterfall. They drank water and had their bath. After half an hour's rest, they proceeded again. Yet another hour too had passed. Then they heard the roar of a tiger. Rodrigues's heart missed a beat. Kevin and Ryan were calm.

'No worry. Tamed ones dispensable with "eats",' Ryan consoled Rodrigues in their jargon. He wanted to test if Rodrigues could catch the meaning.

'Do you get the meaning?' Kevin asked.
'Somewhat,' Rodrigues replied.

'Tell me what you got,' Kevin said.

'It could be "nothing to fear, it's a tamed one",' Rodrigues replied.

'Good, you're getting it,' Kevin said.

'Sensy seems,' Ryan said.

'Got it?' Kevin said to Rodrigues.

'You mean I'm sensible?' Rodrigues asked.

'Yes,' Kevin said.

'Catchy,' Ryan said. 'Got it?' Kevin asked.

' Yes.I learn your jargon faster,' Rodrigues answered.

'Oh! You're right.' Kevin was happy.

Soon they reached a bend.

'This is called Jack Bend. No one who passes this bend can miss a lion or tiger. The animals flock here to drink water from the waterfalls. But no one who passes the bend can forget a sad story too,' Kevin said.

The statement roused an interest in Rodrigues.
'What was that sad story?' Rodrigues asked.

'It was the sad story of our great loss,' Kevin replied.

'Great loss?' Rodrigues asked.

'Yes. Unforgettable one at that,' Kevin replied.

'It was the death of one of our drugged tigers, Jack. You know drugged ones are not mere animals to us. They are like trained soldiers, bent upon protecting their mother country,' Kevin continued.

'Yes, go ahead,' Rodrigues said.

'It was as if our army lost its commander. All the drugged ones came only second to Jack. That's why I told you it was a great loss. It was winter time. One day, the unusual happened. A stray tiger appeared dangerously close to our hut. It was so unusual for a stray one to cross into the "forbidden" area. The moment such a thing happens the drugged ones would at once pounce on it and kill it. But this time the attack was a little delayed. So the intruder tiger escaped on seeing the drugged one. It ran fast for its life. Jack chased it and finally the intruder escaped while the most alert of our drugged ones in its hot chase slipped from the rock overhanging the waterfalls and fell into the water. The water couldn't save it. Its head hit one of the so many rocks sticking out of the water and death was instantaneous. To commemorate its memory, the bend was named after it, and that's how it is called Jack Bend,' Kevin said.

As they neared their dwelling place, the time was nearing midnight. Rodrigues was apprehensive on seeing so many tigers, drugged ones, though. There were four huts. As they entered one of the huts, about six tigers thronged before it. Kevin made them happy and exhilarated by giving them eats. Soon they moved away from the hut but were around keeping watch.

Kevin, Ryan, and Rodrigues had some food. One extra bed was made for Rodrigues. Soon they were all asleep totally lost to the world.

The next morning came. Everyone got up for their morning ablutions. Then they had breakfast. Rodrigues was keen to know more about the place.

'Now who owns this hub?' Rodrigues asked.

'We are not allowed to disclose such details. But we have a network of such hubs. This hub has an added advantage. We manufacture the stuff here,' Ryan replied.

'Oh! Is it so? How do you make it?' Rodrigues asked, slightly excited.

'We're not supposed to reveal such things. But we can give you some harmless information, but never the technical know-how. We keep a drug plantation here and a factory near it. And we can show you around,' Ryan said.

'I'm interested, and when are you going to take me around?' Rodrigues asked.

'Tomorrow,' Kevin replied.

The next day, Rodrigues was taken around the plantation and the factory nearby. Rodrigues plucked a leaf and squeezed it in his hand, and it gave out a heady smell. In the factory, he saw a large number of small plastic bags kept in tiers.

'They are our finished products. They are sent from here to our various outlets. This is a huge establishment,' Kevin said.

'We call our customers pilgrims. We call them disciples also. And they are on a pilgrimage to us for the ethereal experience. We call our hub "The Pleasure Point". Our aim in conducting this business is to spread the message of this rare experience, to make this experience that of the common man. No one born into this world could normally experience this pleasure before he leaves this world. Though each unit is allowed to function independently, we are united under one boss. Our goal is one and the same. But our ways of functioning are different. Each and every hub has an autonomous way of functioning,' Kevin said.

Rodrigues felt Kevin and Ryan were good Samaritans, ready to lend their helping hands to the needy. They were caretakers of the distressed. After chewing the drugs, Rodrigues was happy and a kind of love and respect developed in his mind towards them.

Days passed. Kevin and Ryan went out as usual for fieldwork. In the evening, they returned after the day's work. Sometimes they brought new people. Sometimes they returned without any. This was their routine.

Chapter 33

One day, Kevin and Ryan went out as usual and they never returned. Soon the news reached the hub that they were taken into custody by the police. This was a shock to Rodrigues. So, he had reason to believe that yet another police raid in the Bandipur hub is likely to take place, in pursuance of the confessions by Kevin and Ryan in police custody. He was in jitters. One night, Rodrigues was feeding the tigers when he saw a man in a priest's robe walking towards the hut. He took cover behind a tree so as not to be seen by the man. As he watched him, he could unmistakably place him as the priest who had treated him in his clinic at Coorg..

From the very first occasion of his meeting the priest for treatment, Rodrigues had an inkling that his face was familiar to him but not as a priest. Actually, his priest's robe made him think the resemblance he felt could as well be unfounded. But when he absconded from Vypeen to meet the priest a second time, he had no such inkling as he was so fatigued and was so badly in need of drugs at any cost. But when he saw the priest coming towards the hut, his initial doubt got the better of him. He noticed the priest moved towards the hut as a man who was locally very familiar with the surroundings and directions of the place. Piecing together his information from the police on his way to Coorg to identify the corpse that the police had raided the priest's clinic at Coorg and the priest's presence at the hub at Bandipur, made him think in unmistakable terms that the man in the priest's robe was a masquerader having a criminal background. But for more confirmation he took a trip down memory lane to find out where he had met him first. And the present circumstances aided his probe. Then it occurred to him that the guy was none other than Dick Morasse, the notorious criminal who had absconded after committing the gruesome murder of one Freddie, an employee of the Zenith Distillery, of which he was the lone eyewitness. It was when Rodrigues too was working there as a security personnel. But he couldn't come out in the open to inform the police then, for fear of his dear life. Then his own experience that he gave him drugs as part of his treatment confirmed the guy's criminality.

Seeing the priest, Rodrigues grew more apprehensive that he must be looking for an opportunity to do away with him in connection with Freddie's murder for destroying the only evidence – the only eye witness that he was, whose existence was a perennial threat to his safety. And this could be the reason he came to Bandipur hub where he stayed. If he had escaped the Coorg raid, why had he come straightway to Bandipur itself? He could have gone anywhere in hiding. So Rodrigues thought in all probability the guy must have come to kill him, he having got some clue about his whereabouts. 'Nothing else could be the reason that brought him here. Now, I cannot believe it could be by some strange coincidence he reached Bandhipur, where I live too. So, I must escape from this place now itself. I have no time to waste. Any delay would expose me to Dick and the worse is going to happen,' Rodrigues thought fearfully.

But Rodrigues was unaware of the fact that the priest had recognized him at his first meeting itself at Coorg and had made an attempt on his life by the thug, Reuban. Then the priest dropped the idea on the advice of one of his trusted lieutenants, Robert. One day, the priest called Robert aside and said, 'I seek your advice on an important matter. As you know, it's confidential.'

'Yes, Father, it goes without saying,' Robert replied.

'As you know, the guy who was the only eyewitness to the murder of Freddie of Zenith Distillery, Vypeen, has come to me for treatment. His name is Rodrigues. Now wouldn't he be a potential threat to me if he is alive? I sent our Reuban to make an attempt on his life when he first came to me for treatment. But he failed as four unsuspecting tribes men suddenly appeared on the scene, who were returning from the town after selling their wares, collected from the forest,' the father told him, lowering his voice.

'But, Father, what you did was suicidal, to say the least,' Robert said with concern.

'I wanted to consult you before I decided. But you were away on another mission,' the father replied.

'But you could have waited a bit before jumping into such temperamental decision. You know how such acts would tell upon your well-being? Now you're in disguise. And it's so long that the police couldn't find you out. And recent reports say the case has been shelved as the investigation reached a blind alley and so far so good. Now you shouldn't do anything to invite the police attention. Now the present status quo shouldn't be disturbed by any such act on your part,' Robert said.

'But so far nothing happened. And going by your opinion, I feel the failure of the first attempt is a blessing in disguise for me,' the priest said.

'Yes, Father. But don't forget any time you could be spotted, even if nothing is done by you to invite police attention. Don't be complacent. You should be on your guard endlessly. There is only a thin line between the police finding and not finding you. If you had killed Rodrigues in your first attempt, it would have attracted the police attention to Coorg. And an unmistakable investigation would help the police fix you. Past incidents abound in example when criminals who have escaped police attention have been nabbed in yet another criminal act, and once you're in police custody they would make you confess all your past criminal acts. And soon you would be behind the bars. So take care,' Robert said.

In conformity to the advice of Robert, in whom the priest had firm faith, he dropped the very idea. Rodrigues never knew it was thus he had got another lease of life.

Chapter 34

Rodrigues hadn't to think twice. Though the priest's attempt on his life was never in Rodrigues's knowledge, his decision to escape from the place that night itself was final.

In the dead of night, a man with a bundle of rags was seen walking fast. Frequently, he cast a fearful look back. It made one feel he was escaping from somebody who was following him. He had a beard which was grizzled and unkempt. His hair was long and dishevelled, reaching his shoulders, which was indicative of his having not been to a barber for months. He walked through the jungle for three days and stopped when he came to a small township. He looked out for a place to sleep. He spotted a veranda of a shop. Unloading his bundle, he made a bed with his tattered blanket. Then he casually took out a cigarette butt which he kept in a matchbox and lit it with a lighted matchstick and started smoking. There was a momentary glow in the darkness when he rubbed the matchstick on the matchbox, causing a fire that straggled with a hissing sound. Once again, he looked around for someone watching him. Soon he fell into a fantasy. He pouted his lips in a circle and blew out rings of smoke from his mouth one after another. When he had finished smoking, he was drowsy. Soon he fell on to the spread blanket and was asleep. It was nearing dawn. But he was unaware of it. Then there was a gentle touch on his body. He woke up with a start. He stared at the man standing near him.

'Go away. This is a hotel. It's time for us to start our work.' The man wasn't rude to him. He didn't venture to drive him away with cursing words, as was the wont when a beggar was driven away. He spoke softly. There was compassion in his words. But he could not entertain him there like that. He had to send him away before the early morning customers, who stayed in the lodges around for the night, arrived for their morning coffee or breakfast. The bearded man moved to the veranda of yet another shop nearby, gathering all his paraphernalia. Soon he disappeared into the darkness. After some time, he reappeared.

'Who're you?' the man who had woken him up asked. The bearded man fumbled. No answer issued forth. The man who had woken him up feared that there could be a bomb in his bundle. He asked him to open it, which he promptly did. Having found nothing scary, he asked him to move away.

'I hadn't any food for the past three days. I'm hungry. Please give me something,' the man beseeched.

The hotel manager was a kind man. But he knew what he had asked for was free food. This was against his belief. He or for that matter all the hoteliers had a belief that if the day's first sales was preceded with a free supply of food that day's business would be dull. This made him unhappy. But he was a good soul. So he obliged.

When breakfast was ready, he was served with sumptuous food which the man devoured with gusto. Once he finished the food, he was happy. His haggard-looking eyes gleamed. He looked at the manager of the hotel who had given him food with gratitude. His quivering lips parted and widened as he gave out a wan smile.

The hotelier believed it was his compassion to the needy that had helped him to rise from rags to riches. He had reached Dahana Hulley in Karnataka fifteen years ago. He had been totally broke. It was not his fault. His thought went back to the past and fixed on a particular person by name Ramana. He couldn't say if he was his father. He used to take him around, begging. He ill-treated him. When he grew up, his body had marks of burns. Ramana was a professional beggar. He knew the basics of begging, which was to create sympathy in others by being as humble as possible, by feigning as infirm as possible, by exhibiting running wounds with nauseating puss. It was his special tactics to use children in the aforementioned manner, which he knew would fetch him more money. The boy didn't know anything of his antecedents. The only thing he could remember was that the man called him Bappi. He didn't know if the name was one that was given to him by his parents. If the boy chanced to get an injury on his body, then the man's tendency was to nurse it for the worse. As the boy grew up, he started to flout the man. Then the man started to attack him. Once on such an occasion, the man attacked the boy with a knife. Then he ran away from him. It was thus he reached Dahana Hulley. There he was taken on as a dishwasher in a hotel. The hotel manager was a man who gave importance to neatness and cleanliness. The owner was mighty impressed by the boy's work. He liked him. Soon he was given promotion as the head supplier. By that time, the boy had grown into a full-fledged youth. When the owner fell ill, he knew he had to do something about his business so that it could be continued. He decided to give his daughter to Bappi in marriage, and soon he became the owner of the property.

The beggar was still waiting there. Then the hotelier sensed he needed some money to travel. The bearded man told him he wanted to move to Kochi and that he didn't have money for his bus fare. The kind man bought a ticket for the beggar to travel to Kochi. He boarded a bus called Krishna that plied between Dahana Hulley and Kochi.

As the bus was ready to move, he looked around once again, to see if someone was following him. Soon it moved.

After half an hour, two men reached the spot from where the bus had started. They looked around for the bus. It was obvious they were looking for the bus Krishna that had left for Kochi. There were so many other buses to different destinations, awaiting their time to move. But the one they looked for wasn't there. The small township had a busy bus stand from where buses to different directions started their trips. The men were brothers and were in their military fatigues. But one look at their faces would reveal they were stealthy bullies with criminal intentions. They scoured around. Finally they entered the hotel and ordered their breakfast. One of them was tall and the other was short. It was this that had prompted their parents to name them Tall Boy and Short Boy. A small microphone was hidden in their beards and a small transmitter, beneath their clothes. It was obvious their move was monitored. Then they could communicate to their hub where their boss would be before a receiver and their talk and their whereabouts and activities would be directly monitored by their boss. And the boss could, as well, directly pass his orders as to what they should do, when they were out in the field on a mission. To an outsider, it would seem a normal and natural talk between two friends while their each and every move would be passed on to their headquarters. It was their strategy to make out to the unwary public and passers-by that both of them were talking to each other. Then nothing would look strange.

The manager of the hotel noticed them. Their behaviour roused in him suspicions. He was watching. He listened to their talk. Their voices were muted. So audibility was poor. The manager got off his seat and walked around as if he was watching all the customers to find out if they had any requirement unattended. He found some. Some of the customers were in need of water. Some needed coffee. He urged the responsible servers to be faster. Then he sauntered towards the two men in uniform and asked if they needed anything more. They shook their heads in the negative. Their so leisurely way of eating food showed that eating food was not their intention of visiting the hotel. The manager of the hotel stood near them and feigned as if he was concentrating on something else, while he listened.

'No, the guy couldn't have gone that way. If he did, then he must have been buried in yesterday's landslide with those forty men in the bus,' Tall Boy said.

'But hadn't the earth been removed yesterday itself? It was so reported in the media,' Short Boy asked.

'No. I asked the locals,' Tall Boy replied.

'But remember we're on an important mission. So we can't take things for granted. Our boss is sharp. And we have to be sharper. Then only we could continue to be in his good books,' Short Boy replied.

While they were talking with each other, they never forgot to put off the microphone temporarily, lest the talk between them should reach their boss with whom their transmitter was connected.

'The guy who passed the information was one of the locals coming from the scene. Locals are the best reliable men. They are naive and sincere. They have no airs. If we ask such people about information like what went wrong somewhere, as in this case, or a route to a particular place, they would pour out even the minutest details about it,' Tall Boy said.

'You mean more than the long and short of it?' the short boy asked in a humorous manner.

'Yes. And as if not satisfied with what information they have already given, they would walk alongside and abreast of the slow-moving vehicle, pouring out more information, till the vehicle gains speed and they can no longer keep themselves abreast of the speeding vehicle,' Tall Boy replied.

'See our job is not to believe anyone. Isn't that we were taught by our boss?' Short Boy asked.

'Yes. But it doesn't prevent us from using discriminations,' Tall Boy said.

'If the earth has not been removed from the road blocking the traffic even now, then he must have escaped from here to Kochi as the traffic along that route which goes to Tamil Nadu isn't possible. So the possibility of his going to Tamil Nadu can be ruled out,' Short Boy said.

'Now we have to ask somebody about him,' Tall Boy said.

'It's impossible on two counts. Firstly, he looks a dirty beggar with his unkempt beard and dishevelled hair.

Nobody would ever notice him. Secondly, we're on a secret mission of taking him into custody. So going around and asking people would be risky. People would ask questions about our identity, which we won't be able to reveal. We won't be able to give convincing answers to their questions about us. Then the people would start suspecting us. It's dangerous to create such a situation. Why should we get ourselves trapped by making the purpose of our visit to this place public,' Short Boy said.

'I have an idea. Going by the time of his disappearance, he must have come to this place by nightfall. He must have slept somewhere here. He must have had his breakfast from this hotel, as this is the only one around. If this is true, he must have gone to Kochi by the first bus from here. Then he is sure to reach Kochi by evening. So what I feel is not to get into trouble by going around and asking people. It's safe to go to Kochi directly from here by a taxi instead of wasting our time here. We may be lagging behind by about an hour at the most, which we could make up. A drive faster would help us to make up for the lag. And we could reach Kochi before the bus reached there,' Tall Boy said.

'But it's foolish to move to Kochi without confirming our conjectures,' Short Boy said.

'Then let us ask somebody,' Tall Boy replied.
'Yes, our time is precious,' Short Boy replied.

The hotel manager, overhearing their discussions here and there, reasonably thought in all probability he would be the person to be asked for confirmation of their guesswork. So he slowly sauntered away to the counter. He sat on his chair and started reading a newspaper. He knew the person whom the guys were in search of was the poor man who looked like a beggar, to whom he gave a free breakfast and stood his bus fare to Kochi.

'The hotel manager is the best person who could give us some valuable information,' Short Boy replied.

Then they moved to the manager's counter.

'Excuse me; could you give us some information about somebody who must have visited this hotel for his breakfast this morning?' Tall Boy asked.

'Who is he after all whom you search for? Here so many people come and go. But what's the big idea?' the manager asked.

'He is an escapee from our camp,' Short Boy said.
'How does he look like?' the manager asked.

'He looks black, but not so really. It's his beggar's life that has made him look black. His hair is dishevelled touching his shoulder. His beard is unkempt and grizzled. His overall look is that of a beggar. Going by our calculation, he must have had his breakfast here,' Short Boy replied.

'You said it's his beggar's life that made him look black. So is he a beggar? And then what makes you come here in search of a beggar?' the hotel manager asked.

The question put Short Boy in a fix. He fumbled to give a plausible explanation.

'Yes. He's a beggar who decamped from our camp,' Tall Boy replied.

'Oh! Then you run a beggars' camp? Is it a beggars' training camp or a state meet of the beggars?' the hotel manager asked with a dash of humour in his tone, knowing that they were getting confused. Then he left it at that.

The manager looked as if rummaging through his memory. But he could confirm the person whom the men were after was the guy to whom he had given breakfast and for whom he stood the bus fare. But he felt sorry for him and wanted to save him from the fellows. He was sure the fellows were hoodlums.

'He looks black, but not really. His beggar's life made him look like one,' the manager repeated for confirmation. Then he looked at the guys' faces for some time. The guys were eagerly looking at the manager, hoping for a positive answer.

'Oh! Such a fellow . . . yes,' the manager spoke in a soft voice.

Hearing those words, the faces of the guys brightened. They eagerly looked at his face, hoping the information they wanted would come out of his mouth the next moment.

'Yes, now I remember . . . Distinctly and for sure, the fellow of your description hasn't visited our hotel till this moment.' The manager's reply made the guys' faces sullen. After paying the charges for their food they left. They gathered that the name of the only bus that plied between Dahana Hulley and Kochi was Krishna. Soon they boarded a taxi. The driver was told to overtake the tourist bus Krishna to Kochi, which had started its journey in the morning. The car moved at a breakneck speed.

The hotel manager knew the life of the bearded man was in danger.

'Poor guy! He would be killed by those bullies who seem to me drug peddlers. After all, he is nobody to me and it should be his own worry. But still I can't let it go like that. He must have escaped from the camp, unable to bear the harassment. And the guys who followed him would be here to take him in their custody. And going back to the camp, he will be tortured and perhaps even killed', the hotel manager thought.

The taxi was moving fast towards Kochi.

'The time lag is two hours now. Going by that the normal time taken by a tourist bus to reach Kochi from Dahana Hulley is six hours, we have to make up for the two hours' lag in six hours,' Short Boy said.

'But there is an hour's break for lunch at Vythiri. So the difference comes down to one hour,' Tall Boy said.

'But don't we have to give a similar grace time for our lunch too? We're not machines,' Short Boy said.

'But machines do need rest or they will break down. But it's just the opposite with man. He can forgo a lunch. It would only add to his health going by the modern view of medical science,' Tall Boy replied.

Then the Short Boy moved closer to Tall Boy and lowered his voice to put a word in his ear.

'Then what about the driver? Why should he have to forgo his lunch for our sake?' Short Boy almost whispered into the ear of Tall Boy.

'What you said is correct. So we have to wait till he finishes his lunch. He may be a diabetic patient. He might develop hypoglycaemia. So it's dangerous to ask him to forgo his lunch. In situations like this, we have to consider all such possibilities,' Tall Boy said.

'If we have to stop for the driver's lunch, then we too can have our lunch. The eating time would be the same. I think we can urge the hotel people to treat ours as a special case. Then we would be able to finish our lunch in half an hour,' Short Boy replied.

'I tell you it's very risky,' Tall Boy said.
'What's so much risk in it?' Short Boy asked.

'We cannot be confident of how much urgency others would feel in our case. During the lunch time, the seats would be full. And there would be so many waiting. And there won't be any guarantee the hotel people would accommodate us out of turn. It means we would have to wait a long time for our turn. So there is no guarantee our plan would work. And we cannot wait indefinitely when we have to make up for our time lag and then be at Kochi ahead of the bus,' Tall Boy said.

'Then what should be our plan of action when the bus reaches Kochi?' Short Boy asked.

'Yes, we have to chalk out a foolproof one before we reach Kochi,' Tall Boy said.

'We have to be careful of two things. How could we take him into custody? Should it be immediately when the bus reaches the bus terminal? Or should we follow him and pounce on him in a congenial ambience? What I mean is to catch hold of him when the bus reaches its terminal, has some risks. Our action will be in full view of the public. We're likely to create a scene. The public would gather around. Initially they might take us for some sleuths. But the public have got the right to know who are we to pounce on an unsuspecting man who has just arrived by a bus. There would be his fellow travellers also in the gathering of the public. Then we're bound to reveal our identity to them. And could we do that? Going by what we are, do you think we could ever reveal our real identity?' Short Boy asked.

'No,' Tall Boy replied.

'Then what would be the consequence we have to face if we create a scene? The police would be called in, who would take us in their custody to question. Then it would not only spoil our mission but would bring out all our surreptitious activities going on in Mysore. And remember the narcotic wing of the police is always after us,' Short Boy said.

'But we aren't so much to be afraid of them. Haven't they failed to trace the real man in disguise, except that he is one Fr Lobo Perreira. But they failed to find out that Fr Lobo Perreira was only one of his many facets. He is a well-known masquerader in our circles. Our counterparts in Calcutta, Delhi, Mumbai, and even those from abroad have unanimously agreed he is really an asset to our business. He has a special knack to escape being caught by the sleuths who are after him. What happened to him in Coorg? The sleuths made a surprise rounding up of his clinic, which he could never anticipate at all. The Karnataka and Kerala police did an admirable work in executing their mission. It was foolproof in every respect,' Tall Boy said.

'But one thing, there is none to match Dick Morasse in his deftness in misguiding the sleuths. This is why he could misguide the police that he who owned the clinic at Coorg was a priest by name Fr Lobo Perreira. And this is how he could make the police believe that the guy in the priest's robe who shot himself dead in the Coorg operation was none other than Fr Lobo Perreira, whom they were after. It was actually his confidante Reuban in disguise as the priest. Poor guys had to carry the dead body of Reuban, believing it to be that of Fr Lobo Perreira. But at the same time, Fr Lobo Perreira was on his secret way to the narcotic hub at Bandipur. But the operation was one between equals. The police did a very laudable preparation. They have to be congratulated. But the police who were after Fr Lobo Perreira never knew that he was the much wanted criminal Dick Morasse. All these show he was always a shade above the police, in misguiding them and in making good his escape,' Short Boy said.

'Now the government has declared awards to those participants in the mission of the police force,' Tall Boy added.

'But really the police of Karnataka and Kerala don't deserve any award as the award declared by the government was for nabbing Fr Lobo Perreira and not to carry out an unsuccessful attempt to apprehend him. And in that respect, the Karnataka and Kerala Police have failed. Fr Lobo Perriera is still at large. So they don't deserve any reward,' Short Boy replied.

'I too agree with you in your findings. Yes, what is the purpose in giving awards to those who conducted an abortive raid? Dick Morasse is matchless in his strategy,' Tall Boy agreed.

'Yes, it goes without saying. We have seen it in the Coorg operations. There's none to match Dick Morasse in his deftness in this regard. He could successfully make the police believe that the dead in the priest's robe at Coorg, was none other than Fr Lobo Perreira, whom they were after. Even then he could keep his real identity of Dick Morasse intact and untraceable by the police,' Short Boy said.

'Wasn't it the lack of proper comprehension on the part of the police to take into account every probability of the enemy's move?' Tall Boy asked.

'I don't get what you mean by every probability,' Short Boy said.

'Here the police failed to believe the probability of a wider spectrum of strategies and techniques that could be used by Dick, going by his shrewdness and cunningness. Firstly, the police failed to conceive that the priest who dealt in drugs could in all probability be a notorious criminal in disguise. Then they thought there could be only one priest among the drug peddlers, but failed to conceive of the possibility of more than one in disguise as a priest. So when they saw the dead body of the priest they conclusively took it to be that of Fr Lobo Perreira,' Tall Boy replied.

'In this case the false belief of the police made them complacent for days on end. And it is this complacency that failed the police in making a reasonable inquiry in finding the possibilities of their assessment going wrong. And this gave enough time for Dick to make good his escape,' Short Boy said.

'Poor police guys had to carry the corpse, believing it to be that of Fr Lobo. The police team on the Coorg mission is on cloud nine, wrongly believing they had achieved their mission. They are rejoicing and celebrating as if their mission was a success, as if theirs was a big haul – the one for which they had worked day in and day out, employing all their strategies in their armoury. They believed they had a better strategy. But knowing the strategy of enemies better is more important to win a battle. And that's our technique. In this aspect, they failed. Poor guys! Pity them. And it is only for us that the secret of Dick Morasse is known. Now the police guys have yet to find out his hideout first and then make another year's preparations to nab him. And if they succeeded in their yet another exhaustive and foolproof mission, then only they would realise that Fr Lobo and Dick Morasse are one and the same. Meanwhile, he would escape from there too. No one can ever imagine how Dick is respected by our men and how strong and wide our network is. And who is responsible for the spread of drugs all over India and abroad? It's nothing but his organising capacity in hiding. In fact, the person I feel, the most deserving for the award is none other than Dick Morasse, who showed better deftness and dexterity in fooling a well-trained, well-prepared, and well-equipped police force of

Kerala and Karnataka. Now it will take time before the police and the public coming to know of Dick's grand escape from Coorg. Another of his tactics is he takes special care not to make his face familiar to others. It aids his masquerading. Going by the past experience, the police could, at the most, spring a surprise on him by their secret movements. But none could touch him. And he would fool everybody and escape. They had spent their time and money for months on end to be foolproof in the mission only to get themselves fooled finally. But to Dick, his dexterity needed only a moment to escape and make all the long preparations of the Kerala and Karnataka police fall through,' Tall Boy said.

'We have sidetracked too much from our topic of discussion. We have to take a decision sooner,' Short Boy said.

The car was moving at breakneck speed. Soon there were signs of an approaching town. They couldn't overtake the bus. In ten minutes, the car reached the town of Vythiri. They stopped at a hotel. They went inside and ordered lunch and they made their urgency known to the manager. There was no seat to spare. But the manager was a shrewd businessman who believed in the principle 'make hay while the sun shines'. He arranged lunch for them in his private resting room. There were not enough chairs. But they were ready to make do with it. It was no problem for them. If anything time was their bother. They finished and came out in twenty minutes. The driver had moved to the car.

'Did the tourist bus by name Krishna for Kochi stop here for lunch?' Tall Boy asked.

'Yes, they came here had lunch and left,' the manager replied.

'How long will it take from here to Kochi?' Short Boy asked.

'Normally two more hours,' the manager replied.
'Now, when did the bus leave here?" Tall Boy asked .

"They left here half an hour ago. Now the time being 2.30 p.m., the bus would reach Kochi bus terminal at the Durbar Hall ground around 4 pm. And the difference in the running time between our car and the bus is half an hour. So we have to speed up so as to reach the terminal before 4 p.m., to be more on the safer side.This means we must reach the terminal by 3.30 pm, in one hour' Tall Boy made a mental calculation.

'Could you speed up the car a little more so as to reach Kochi by 3.30 Pm?' Tall Boy asked the driver as he boarded the car.

'Sir, it's no problem, we will reach kochi in an hour. I will adjust the speed accordingly' the driver replied.

The car zoomed forward. The driver looked at his watch and made a mental calculation.

The car was racing faster. About forty five minutes' drive, they saw a bus negotiating a curve.

'It could be the one we're after,' Short Boy whispered. Tall Boy nodded in agreement. Then they had some hasty secret discussion in each other's ears. Finally they came to a decision. Then they talked no more. When the car negotiated a bend, the bus was right in front of the car. The name 'Krishna' was written on it for their confirmation. They looked at the illuminated moving names of the destinations of the bus on its back glass. It was Dahana Hulley to Kochi. This cleared their doubt. Soon the car made short work of the bus's speed by overtaking it. The speed of the car was such that in minutes it negotiated yet another curve and the bus disappeared from their view as if it was going back. Tall Boy and Short Boy were watching through the rear view mirror, to see if the bus appeared again in the mirror, for it would mean the bus was speeding up. And in that case, there was the possibility of the bus overtaking the car and soon it would be off in a flash. To them, it was a critical situation, but not so to the driver. So they had to be vigilant not to allow such a thing to happen. But the driver seemed to be well aware of the passengers' need. The speed of the car was such that the bus couldn't come anywhere near it, since it had overtaken the bus. The car reached the bus terminal in advance. The time was exactly 3.30 pm. The driver was asked to park the car at a suitable distance and to wait in it, which he did.

Tall Boy and Short Boy looked at their watches and found the bus would not reach them before 3.45 pm and they felt relaxed. Then they just walked a few yards away from their waiting car. It was for passing the information to their hub. Time ticked away. The arrival of the bus was nearing. They looked at their watch once again. Soon the bus they were waiting for made its appearance and entered the terminal compound for its final stop. The time was 4.00 pm. They hastily moved towards the bus. The passengers were coming out one after another. And the last man too alighted from the bus. But the bearded man was not there. The two men, surprised at the sudden turn of events, entered the bus to find out if someone was sleeping inside the bus but found none. Their surprise changed to embarrassment and confusion. They were at a loss to find out what had gone wrong and where.

Soon, they too came out of the bus. As soon as their feet touched the ground, their embarrassment and confusion turned into shock when they realized they were surrounded by a ring of policemen in plains from the narcotic cell at Kochi. They took them, their waiting car, and its driver into custody. A policeman took the driver's seat, and they all proceeded to the office of the Narcotic Cell of the Kerala Police, near the Kerala High Court, Kochi.

The informant was none other than the manager of the Hotel Prasanth at Dehanahully who sensed danger to the life of the bearded man to whom he gave free breakfast and stood his busfair to cochin.

Chapter 35

Before reaching the Durbar Hall ground bus terminal, the bus had stopped at the Kerala High Court boat jetty from where the boats to Vypeen started. But as his mind was vaguely engaged in the thoughts of how to earn a living, Rodrigues didn't notice the bus had stopped at the High Court Boat Jetty point. But he realised his mistake later. So he decided to get off the bus at the KSRTC jetty which was the next stop before the terminal.

As soon as Rodrigues alighted from the bus, he started walking back towards the Kerala High Court Boat Jetty. Regarding the money needed for his drugs, he didn't have to worry for one year. He had enough stock to last him for a year, which he had stolen from Bandipur.

'I must have been removed from the company's muster roll for long absence. The owner might have appointed a new one, in my place. If this is so, there's no question of my getting a job. I'm not experienced in any other job, so no chance of my getting a job. Then how can I pull on?'. He was in a dilemma. Rodrigues pulled out a packet which contained drugs. He took a bit of it.

As he was worried about his future, his mind suddenly reminded him of his family and how they had pulled on in his absence. He felt it was not much of his worry. He felt no compunction. He was concerned about his own future.

Everybody he passed, on his way, looked unfamiliar. None seemed to have recognised him.

'It's my change in appearance that made me a stranger in my own native place. It is as if I'm alone in a crowd,' Rodrigues thought. The drug he took started to work. He felt high.

Chapter 36

As he moved forward, passing the hotel Sea Lord, two persons were watching him. 'Look! Who is the man with the beard?' one of them asked the other.

'He looks worn out due to starvation. Could be a beggar, in all probability,' the other man replied.

'No, you can't jump into conclusions. His face seems familiar to me,' the first man said.

'I'm sure something is wrong with your eyes. His face is not familiar to me,' the other man said.

'The problem could be with your eyes. That's what I feel,' the first man replied.

'You are making a fuss of everything. Even if he is familiar to us, why bother about him? Let him go his way,' the other man said.

'No. Let us not leave him like that. The guy is not a beggar. He is a man who is very significant to us,' the first man said.

'Significant in which way?' the other man asked.

'You won't believe if I reveal who he seems to me,' the first man said.

'I'll believe only if you talk sense,' the other man said. 'Then don't you believe I'm a person who talks sense?' the first man asked.

'No man can talk sense always. That's what I feel,' the other man said.

'You mean, sometimes men talk nonsense too?' the first man asked.

'Yes,' the other man replied.

'But does it mean that even if I speak sense, if I'm not able to convince you, you would say I speak nonsense?' the first man asked.

'But I feel when you get convinced, I too would get convinced,', the other man said.

'But if you don't get convinced of what I'm convinced, then you can't say I speak nonsense,' the first man said . . .

'Oh! Forget it. We aren't here to argue. Tell me who is he to you,' the other man asked.

'I'm sure he is our Rodrigues,' the first man replied.
'Oh! What I guessed is correct. You're off your nuts.

How can a dead man come alive after some time? Hadn't he been murdered at Coorg? And Mildred and Maxwell identified the corpse. We all attended the burial too. Now you say the guy is Rodrigues,' the other man said.

'Anyway, he is not far away from us. Now he has crossed the Rainbow Bridge on the Marine Drive. Let's walk a little faster before he disappears from view,' the first man said.

'But you can as well expect him to stop at the High Court Boat Jetty to board one of the boats, if he's the guy of your guess,' the other man said.

'But if he isn't, he might pass the jetty point and walk straight or turn right and go eastward along the Banerjee Road, or there is the possibility of his taking a turn back, in which case we are sure to bump into him. In that case, he's just an evening stroller, like many of those whom we passed,' the other man said.

'In any case, there's no harm in increasing our pace,' the first man urged.

They walked faster. They saw the bearded man sauntering forward some distance ahead of them. Soon he stopped and turned to the parapet of the Marine Drive and sat on it. It was a kind of blessing in disguise for the two men. They reached the place where he was sitting. They too sat on the parapet near him. They watched him for a second. The bearded man, sensing some danger that some spies would pounce on him any time and from anywhere, got up and started walking fast. The other two men followed at a faster pace, to keep him in view so as to prevent his escape. The bearded man increased his pace a little more. Having no other way to stop him, the first man contrived a plan.

'Please stop. We want to talk to you. We're your friends,' he shouted.

Hearing this, the bearded man started running. Then the two men chased him too. The bearded man stumbled on a small boulder and fell. This was quite unexpected, and the two men had to put a sudden stop to their progress so as not to stumble over him and fall. They caught hold of him and helped him to his feet. He was shivering in fear.

'Aren't you Rodrigues?' the first man asked, smiling. The bearded man asked a counter question. This mode of opening up a talk was that of the underworld men. As they were always in hiding, the first lesson the novices of the underworld were taught during their training was 'never to reveal anything, even to your friends'. They were taught to take strangers as sleuths in plain clothes or police informers. So as part of the experience received from the drug mafia the bearded man asked a counter question instead of answering first the question put to him.

'You're Roger?' the bearded man asked a counter question.

'Yes, I'm Roger.'

'And you're King?' the bearded man asked the other. 'Yes, I am King.'

They couldn't believe their eyes. They hugged each other.

'We should not talk here. Let's go to your house,' Roger said.

'Yes,' Rodrigues replied with some diffidence.

Then they walked towards the High Court Boat Jetty. The last boat had moved out of the jetty. Roger called it back. The crew reluctantly turned the boat and anchored at the jetty. They all boarded and soon the boat was off. Fifteen minutes passed. The boat reached the Vypeen Jetty. They all got off the boat and walked towards Rodrigues's house. Despite the pleasure he should have had on meeting his friends after a long time, Rodrigues was in a pensive mood. He was thinking of his future. Then he looked at Roger.

'As my friends, you must find out a job for me,' Rodrigues said weakly. He knew he had no right to tell even to his friends to get him a job, using their good offices. He had created a bad name. In their eyes too, he had turned an unreliable man.

'Who would vouch for the good conduct of a person whose ways are unsure? Who knows he wouldn't make himself scarce, as he did before,' Roger and King soliloquised the same way.

'Where can you get a job? Who will give you a job? Do you think your antecedents are satisfactory to ensure you a job?' Roger asked.

'I have nothing to boast except that I was a disciplined worker so long as I was a worker in the distillery. Can you deny that?' Rodrigues said.

'Our agreement or denial doesn't matter in this context. You have earned a lot of bad names as an unsteady man. Haven't you proved it by your own conduct?' King asked.

'Doesn't the fact that I was a disciplined worker give me an added advantage for my job prospects?' Rodrigues asked a counter question.

'But what about your long absence from the company without any leave? Wasn't it an act of gross indiscipline on your part? This aspect goes very much against you. But you are ignoring this vital point and your views are not in conformity with what a reasonable man would think of you. And your job prospects depend upon what I mentioned above. And do you think it would be supportive of your getting a job? What have you to say about my question? In matters like this, you should never think of your own plus points. A third party would never take into consideration such things. This is because they don't have to bother about you. There are umpteen job seekers who are better qualified and well disciplined than you. So you cannot expect the owner to think in your favour always. This you have to bear in mind. But all told, I think you're lucky in a way,' Roger said.

'How come?' Rodrigues's inquisitiveness doubled. A ray of hope burst in his mind.

He was actually aware of those facts which Roger and King had said. But his job was a question of his livelihood, which made him think of everything in his favour.

'In your absence, Maxwell got your job and he is still continuing it. Now he has passed his bachelor's degree in education and is in search of a teacher's job. If he leaves, the owner might consider you. Considering your present wayward ways, the owner might as well take on a more disciplined person even if Maxwell opts for leaving the job. Then also you have no chance. But everything depends upon your luck,' Roger said.

'Now this could be a fight between the father and the son, if Maxwell opts to continue his job, till he gets a teacher's job,' King said.

'Yes, in all probability,' Roger said.

'Normally, it could never turn out to be a problem between the father and the son,' King replied.

'But is there any normal relationship between the father and the son?' Roger asked.

'That's what I too am thinking of. This question of strained relationship between the father and the son is likely to spoil Rodrigues' prospects, even though it's a matter between the father and the son,' King said.

'For the past one year, he had discarded his family. He never bothered how his family lived. Where did they get the money to make ends meet? Who funded the son's education? All these questions weren't his worry. Shouldn't he have been one who voluntarily addressed all these questions as a husband and a father, staying at home? Then what did he do? He left his family high and dry and was at large for the past one year. He never cared for his son's education.

In fact, his son had to keep him in good humour for the money he needed for his education. Once Rodrigues had angrily warned him he would stop funding his education. Would any loving father say so? He had no interest in his son's welfare or for that matter in the welfare of his family. Then what right has he to expect any loving gesture from his son? I don't think he would quit the job for the sake of his wayward father. We have to wait and see,' Roger said.

'But the decisive factor is our employer. If he has his old affinity to Rodrigues still in his mind, he would opt for him despite his wayward habits. Then even if Maxwell is in his good books, the fact that he is soon to leave the profession for his much awaited teacher's job would be a plus point in favour of Rodrigues. But there is no point in racking our brain on the issue,' Roger replied.

'But even that isn't a plus point to Rodrigues. What's the guarantee that Rodrigues wouldn't leave his job and go away?' King asked.

Rodrigues was in a pensive mood, in his own world of thoughts. He and his friends were heading for Rodrigues's house. His mind was boggled and he was not in a mood to take active part in the discussions going on between his friends. They reached home. Mildred came to answer the doorbell. She invited Roger and King in, but ignored the dirty, emaciated beggar-looking third man.

'Do you know who he is?' Roger asked Mildred.

'I don't know him. But why is he here? Who brought him here? Tell him to get lost,' she told Roger, without pausing for a breather.

Roger laughed. Then unmindful of what Mildred had said of the stranger, he took the initiative to invite him in.

He was asked to sit down, which he obeyed. Mildred didn't much approve of Roger's gesture. She stared at the stranger. Her thoughts went down memory lane. With a shock, she realized then. She couldn't believe her eyes. Unbelievable! She walked up and down the room.

Then she stopped and stared at the bearded man once again.

'Oh no! It's not so. It's not so. I'm sure. It's not so. But who is he? From where did you get him? I will never believe something like a dead man coming alive. It's impossible.' Mildred looked as if she had lost her ability to keep her emotions at bay. She cried and then laughed and then turned gloomy.

Roger and King were watching her. Soon they heard the doorbell again.

This time King went to answer it. He opened the door. It was Maxwell. He came in and wishing Roger and King he took a seat. Mildred was by that time calm, having been forced to reconcile with the unbelievable reality. Then Maxwell noticed the bearded man who was silent, his head hung. It didn't take much for Maxwell to identify his father. But he wasn't happy. He thought his mother's miseries which he thought had ended once for all were soon to recur. He thought of the bad days ahead of him because of his father's presence. He recognised him as his father, but his mind couldn't accept him. He was so agitated.

'This is the end of the joyful days for me. As for my mother, she may be ready to accept him, going by her peculiar views on marital life. But I can never agree to her views,' Maxwell thought desperately.

He looked at his mother. She was nonchalant now. Now she was more worried about how her husband and son would get along. Then the problem of getting a job for him troubled her. With regards to his job prospects, she had nothing to pin her hopes on.

'Then whose was the dead body we identified? If the body was that of another, how could we spot the wedding ring inscribed "Mildred" on the finger of the corpse? There was some mix-up somewhere,' Maxwell thought.

Rodrigues was unaware of the turn of events after his departure. So he couldn't understand the confusion among his friends, wife, and son about him.

'Now what do we see? A dead man coming alive,' Roger said.

'Something went wrong somewhere,' King added. 'Our identification of the dead body was wrong,'

Maxwell said.

'No. It can never go wrong. If you assess our identification was wrong, what have you to tell about my wedding ring inscribed "Mildred" on the corpse's finger?' Mildred asked.

Roger and King too were in confusion. They thought of informing the police of Rodrigues's return. They told it to Maxwell and Mildred.

'But we should not jump to conclusions. Informing the police is something that requires detailed thinking,' Maxwell said.

'What makes you think so?' Roger asked.

'What makes you think of telling the police?' Maxwell asked a counter question to Roger.

'I feel the police could find out the answers to our questions. They're experienced and trained,' Roger said.

'But we must think from our point – the consequences we have to face if we inform the police. Now my mother, my father, and I have escaped being framed in the drug case. But informing the police that my father is alive makes the case more and more complicated,' Maxwell said.

'Then the police cannot be blamed if they implicate Rodrigues in the murder of that person. The wedding ring is vital and undeniable evidence to establish the connections between the deceased and Rodrigues. But how come the ring on the finger of the deceased?' Mildred asked.

'Only Rodrigues could answer our questions,' Roger replied.

'So the question of hastily informing the police would affect Rodrigues adversely. And what is going to happen is, they would immediately arrest him and put him behind the bars. Then he will not get even a bail because the crime is so serious,' King added.

'Now the police are under the impression that the corpse was that of my father and that he is no more. But if we inform them that he has come back alive, then their immediate duty will be to find out whose dead body was buried as that of my father. This is a serious question which they cannot ignore and keep themselves away from,' Maxwell asserted his view once again.

'How could we inform the police? But how we couldn't?' Mildred asked.

Rodrigues was silent, thinking of his job. He wasn't bothered about the serious problem caused by his surprise return.

If there hadn't been the question of the dead body with the wedding ring of Mildred's name, Rodrigues's coming back wouldn't have any significance. And if at all the police was informed of his homecoming, they wouldn't attach any importance to it. At the most, they would arrest and produce him before the magistrate to record his existence and then the court would let him go free. But the case was not that simple. How come his wedding ring on the finger of the corpse wrongly identified as that of Rodrigues? Then definitely, there would be a connection between the deceased and Rodrigues. But his death was confirmed long before by identifying the wedding ring. Rodrigues who was to answer this important question could not recollect properly how all this had happened.

Everyone looked at Rodrigues rather instinctively, though they all knew he wasn't in a position to recollect it.

'Where were you all these days?' Maxwell asked in an effort to jog his father's memory of past events.

'I was in Bandipur,' Rodrigues replied.
'Bandipur! How come?' Roger asked.
There was no reply from Rodrigues.

'This is not an easy thing as we thought. It seems we have to do some investigations – how he happened to be in Bandipur or if he was in Coorg really,' Roger said.

'It gives me an inkling that he had murdered somebody and we buried that guy's corpse. Drug addicts sometimes turn murderers,' King said.

'But why must they sometimes turn murderers? Going by my information, of course based on rumours, grapevine, and media reports, I believe they are a kind of docile, sleepy people in a fantasy land,' Maxwell asked.

'No. You're young and your information isn't correct. I have seen so many addicts, and many of them turn murderers or sometimes they even commit suicide,' Roger replied.

'But how come?' Maxwell asked.

'When they are hard up for money to buy drugs, they resort to anything to get money to buy drugs,' Roger said.

'Then they are kind of frustrated lot. And out of frustration and out of urgency, sometimes they resort to a kind of begging. There have been instances when someone refusing to pay money was killed by an addict. In some cases, the addicts committed suicide. Their recklessness was well brought out by an incident some years ago. An addict had no money to buy drugs. In his frustration, he pierced his index finger deep into his eye socket and scooped out his right eye. So the drug addicts are not always docile people in fantasy, as you might think. They are in fantasy when they have money to buy enough drugs. But they are ferocious when they are short of drugs,' King dished out his better information.*

Everyone was in a fix. Their discussions came to a stop. But still they had to go forward and find out solutions for these riddles. They all came to the conclusion that only Rodrigues could answer the question of the wedding ring. Soon they all parted to meet the next day to grill Rodrigues. They all thought it was a Herculean task to bring to Rodrigues's memory the story of the wedding ring.

Chapter 37

The next morning, they met at Rodrigues's house. Everybody was present and was anxious to find out the truth, failing which would create so many complications.

Roger ventured to start . . .

'I would like to ask you some important questions. Please listen,' he started.

'Tell me how many times you have visited Coorg. Please take your time and try to give your answers correctly,' Roger asked.

'Only once,' Rodrigues replied.

'No. Don't you remember you visited Coorg first with Mildred and Maxwell?' Roger asked.

Rodrigues looked blank. Then he stared at the sky for some time. His face had assumed an expression that showed he could recollect. He looked at Roger and said, 'Yes.'

'Then didn't you make another visit to Coorg alone?' Roger asked.

Rodrigues looked as if he was recollecting; his eyes looked meaninglessly at the sky for some time. Then as if he remembered . . . he looked at Roger.

'Yes, I paid a second visit to Coorg. Then I was alone,' Rodrigues replied.

'Where did you get money for your journey?' Roger asked.

'It was no problem. I had enough money for my travel,' Rodrigues replied.

'You mean you had enough money for your bus charge?' Roger asked.

Again, there was that blank look for some time. Then he said, 'Yes.'

'But didn't you take treatment at the priest's clinic?' Roger asked.

'Yes,' Rodrigues replied.

'How long did you stay in Coorg?' Roger put forth the question in his effort to find out if he was in Coorg only during his long absence from Vypeen or had visited Bandipur.

'I don't remember exactly,' Rodrigues replied. 'Take your time and find out,' Roger said.

Rodrigues lapsed into thought. He took some time to answer. He seemed to be making some mental calculations with effort. Finally he said, 'I don't remember . . .'

'You think it over. Take your time,' Roger replied. 'It could be a week or so,' Rodrigues said.

'Where did you get the money for the treatment and for your food and stay? Did anybody meet your expenses?' Roger asked.

'No, I had my own money,' Rodrigues replied.

'Your own money! Where did you get it?' Roger asked. Rodrigues was pensive for some time. He looked blank

again . . . And then he ventured to answer.

'I pledged my ring to a money lender,' Rodrigues replied.
'Wasn't it your wedding ring inscribed "Mildred"?'
Roger asked.

'Yes. My wedding ring, my wedding ring,' Rodrigues
repeated.

'Don't you remember his name?' Roger asked.

Again the blank look . . . He looked as if he was recollecting
the name . . .

'Yes. He was one Ryphen,' Rodrigues replied.

'Then the corpse we buried here was that of Ryphen, no
doubt,' Roger said.

Though the mystery was solved, to Maxwell, Mildred,
Roger, and King, it was like jumping from fire to frying pan.
They couldn't keep Rodrigues in hiding for long. They had to
take him to the police and regularise the records. Then the
police would have to find out the identity of the deceased,
whom they had buried at Vypeen thinking that the corpse was
that of Rodrigues. And this would create further questions,
like who killed Ryphen. Then they would have to establish
that the wedding ring had no connection with the murder. There
were so many problems, so many hard knots that couldn't be
disentangled easily. In all probability, Mildred and Rodrigues
would have to be behind the bars till the case was proved.

Maxwell was racking his brain all the while. Then he came
up with a solution.

'How about seeking the help of that police officer whom
we bribed once?' Maxwell asked.

'Then we might have to pay through our nose to satisfy
them, as the case is more serious,' Mildred replied.

'That's right,' Roger agreed.

'But it's a very serious problem. We have to do whatever is possible to exonerate Rodrigues and Mildred from being framed as the accused in the murder of Ryphen,' King said as an afterthought.

'But going to the police is just like getting ourselves trapped,' Roger said.

'But we cannot hide Father from the police for long. We are duty bound to bring him before the law and get him exonerated. We cannot abstain from it. If we fail, the consequences would be serious. And we are not to take any such risks. But we will meet the police officer and reveal the real story and ask him to save us,' Maxwell said.

The next day, Maxwell made secret enquiries to find out if the police officer who had saved them from the other case was still in charge. There was a ray of hope in his mind when he learnt the same officer was still in charge.

Chapter 38

One day, Maxwell and Mildred went to meet the officer. He was in his office. Seeing them, the officer was happy.

'Come in. Take your seats,' he said.

'God is omniscient. He puts people in a quandary and brings them to me. Only when you are in trouble you come to me. And it's that way I can also solve my problems. I'm a firm believer in God and I know he always lends his helping hand to me. Now I'm badly in need of some money. And you came to me as a godsend. I can sense something wrong has happened to you, which brought you to me, and you need my help . . .,' he laughed heartily.

Maxwell noticed his left upper canine tooth was missing. He was sure it had happened since his last meeting with him.

In his happy mood, the officer jocularly mentioned this to Maxwell – the story behind the loss without Maxwell's asking.

'Do you know how it happened?' the officer asked, showing the gap of his missing tooth.

Maxwell was the least interested. So he kept quiet.

'I lost it in an encounter with a criminal. Then I had enough money to fill the gap with a golden tooth. But it turned out to me a blessing in disguise. I made it a detachable one and it serves a double purpose for me. Whenever I'm cash-strapped, I pledge it with a money lender, and when I get money from people like you, I release the pledge. And I would, as well, advise you: When you have money, invest it in gold before it drains off. Then it would help you when you are cash-strapped. It's a lesson I learnt over the years. But now as you have come to me, I suppose you have a problem. And the money to release the pledge is soon to come my way. I'm always lucky in this respect. God is graceful. Praise the Lord.' He laughed again.

'Well, what are you up to?' the officer continued.

'We have a problem,' Maxwell replied.

'I know that. That's why God has brought you here. God is always kind to me. He brings people to me to solve their problems and that way that of mine too. Then they disappear as if vanished into thin air. Then new ones come to me. I firmly believe that it's nothing but the handiwork of the Almighty. I'm a firm believer in God. I pray to God to conduct me well. And so far not even a single prayer of me has gone unanswered.' The officer laughed again.

Maxwell and Mildred didn't feel like laughing. They were obsessed with their problem.

'Now our problem is the corpse we had buried here some time ago as my father's is not his. We identified the body going by the wedding ring of my mother on the finger of the corpse.'

'Yes, I do remember the incident, and so what?' the police officer asked.

'Now after so many months, he has come back,' Maxwell said.

'Yes. Go ahead . . .,' the police officer said.

'Now we are in a quandary. How can you help us?' Maxwell asked.

'If this was a case of a missing person coming back, it's simple. But this case is complicated. It's attached to murder. If the corpse isn't Rodrigues's, the wedding ring plays an important role to find the murderer. Then your mother Mildred too would be framed as the accomplice. So your problem is you all want to escape from the trap, including your father, Rodrigues, isn't it?' the officer said.

'Yes, sir,' Maxwell replied.

The officer soon lapsed into a pensive mood for some time. He twiddled his fingers, crooning a number. Then a smile appeared on his lips.

'My long experience in the police service has taught me lessons. People would come to me to be saved. You know, I'm not hard-hearted like many of the officers. I'm compassionate, as you already know. Now we the compassionate ones among the officers have secretly developed four methods to save those who come to us to be saved, which are called "detachment", "attachment", "removal", and "drowning".' He laughed.

'In your case, I'm to use all these methods because it's a complex one, as your father believed to have been dead has come back. The questions as to whose body was buried as that of your father and how come the wedding ring of your mother on the finger of the corpse assume significance. The inquest report also is there to make things complicated. But I think I can save you. I'll detach the several causes and make them independent ones as if having no connections with each other. This is called "detachment". Then your father is to be attached to the simple case as an absconder. This is "attachment". For the technique of attachment to be successful, I have to resort to the technique of "removal".

The inquest report is to be removed from the file. When removal takes place, the technique of "drowning" comes into play automatically. This works when we drown the file containing the remaining papers into the unwieldy mass of files of discontinued or finished case files, which are destined to gather dust in our records room. A case showing the minimum cause of action is to be charged against your father and it's that of an absconder. We would produce him before the magistrate who would set him free. As the inquest report is removed from the file, there is no question of implicating your mother for the cause of the wedding ring on the finger of the unidentified corpse,' the police officer explained.

'Then wouldn't there be an inquiry from your higher-ups about the fate of the case? Wouldn't there be cross-checking and things like that?' Maxwell asked.

'Who is afraid of cross-checking? Or who is bothered of cross-checking? So many cases were similarly re-investigated and all of them were mere farce. And mind you, if anyone ventures to take the probe seriously he is sure to reach a blind alley with no breakthrough. And no one could ever find such files from among the jumble of unwieldy mass of files in our records room. This is how "drowning" takes place. Sometimes there will be a public outcry, finding fault with the local police who investigate the case. They demand the case be handed over to the crime branch for a fair deal. When they too cannot find a breakthrough, there would be yet another public outcry that the case be investigated by the CBI, as the last resort. Finally, the CBI fails too,' the officer explained.

'Wouldn't someone from a special investigation team find it out from the jumble of files?' Maxwell asked.

'Who is bothered about such things? No one is interested in stirring a hornet's nest. If anyone does, we would retaliate in the same fashion when he too is placed in a similar situation. I tell you none is a saint. Then an officer who ventures to undertake such a task is very well aware of its futility. And that reminds me, once there was an inquiry to find out the file of a case. The investigating officer, a handsome and sincere man, traced the hiding place of the file to our records room that was full of dust. None of us joined him. So he ventured to enter the room all by himself and searched among the jumble of files. After half an hour, we could hear a wheezing from inside. Soon he came out, his face swollen beyond recognition due to dust allergy. He was wheezing like an asthmatic patient. Then he had to go on leave for a month for treatment,' the officer said.

'Coming to our point, what's the next step on my part?' Maxwell asked.

'It's not your worry at all. Leave it to us. So bring your father to me tomorrow. I will produce him before the court and he will be set free as an absconder, pure and simple. And mind you, I'm resourceful. And you know, what is the reward for my being resourceful? It's nothing but so many sources of money that come my way,' the officer replied.

Maxwell was eager to know how much the officer would demand. Going by the officer's statements, this was a serious problem. So he knew he would be demanding a large amount. But he wanted the officer to quote it.

'Sir, you know our financial position. Now tell me what would be the minimum you expect from us?' Maxwell asked.

'You know I'm a man of compassion. And that's why I do all these favours for the needy. I could be strict and un-obliging.

Then what would be your fate? You would be behind the bars. Or you might even have a tryst with the noose. The offence is that serious. Now considering the gravity and complications of the present problem, I would like to up the ante a little but it would be affordable to you. When I fix the amount I also think if it suits your pocket. As you know, I'm not a cut-throat. Presently, my fee is nothing but a paltry sum of Rs. 1,00,000 and not a bean more or not a bean less,' the officer said.

Maxwell had a shock. He thought of bringing down the stake.

'How much your good self could come down?' Maxwell asked.

'You know the gravity of the situation you're in?' the officer countered.

'Yes, sir, I'm fully aware of it,' Maxwell replied.

'I'm a man of scruples. The amount quoted by me is the minimum. Think of the situation if I don't help you. You must not think of the amount alone. You should compare it with the benefits you're getting. And you must as well think of how kind I am to you, when I undertake to save you from this stalemate. But I'm compassionate. I cannot stand the tears of people in difficulties. I'm here to wipe their tears. Just as my heart is fixed on saving you, the amount I should get too is fixed. And it's one lakh and not a bean more or not a bean less,' the officer replied.

'It's part of the stride,' Maxwell thought. Mildred and he walked home.

Reaching home, Roger and King were waiting for them to know the results. Maxwell recounted what had been transpired between him and the officer.

'We cannot say anything about the amount demanded by the officer in such cases. The amount may be exorbitant. But I'm sure he won't come down. And if the money reaches his hands, I'm sure he won't let you down also. And the only remedy is to raise the amount somehow, pay it at your earliest, and get yourself out of the trap. So don't waste time thinking about how to get him round for a lesser amount. It will not work,' Roger said.

'I think Maxwell may ask our employer Ramsay, for some money to tide over the difficult situation. As you're in his service and as you're in his good books, he would advance the amount. So you meet him today itself,' King opined.

King's opinion was accepted by all. Maxwell proceeded to meet Ramsay, who was in his office.

'Come in, be seated,' Ramsay said, seeing Maxwell.

'Thank you, sir.' Maxwell did as he was told to do.

'Well, what can I do for you?' Ramsay asked.

Maxwell described him of his predicament in detail.

'Oh! Is it so? I feel sorry for the problem you're in.

But I think I could help you. When do you want the money?' Ramsay asked.

'At the earliest, that's what the police officer said,' Maxwell replied.

He opened his safe and gave the amount in cash. Maxwell was so grateful for his largesse. He heaved a sigh of relief. He had never expected the problem could be solved so easily. He walked home. Reaching home, he told Roger and King about the success of his mission. All were happy. The next morning, Maxwell, Mildred, and Rodrigues proceeded to meet the police officer. He was in his office. Seeing them, his face brightened. Soon the money changed hands.

'Now you don't have to bother. Nobody would come after you. Forget all about the problem. It's solved forever. The question of the wedding ring on the hands of the corpse is solved as I removed the inquest report from our files. Then about Rodrigues, his offence is a simple one of an absconder from Vypeen. I would produce him before the magistrate today itself and set him free. No problem. Don't bother about it any more. I'm here. So be happy,' the officer said in an assuring tone. Rodrigues was produced before the magistrate, and by noon he was set free. Then they all walked home.

Chapter 39

Maxwell had passed his degree in education in the first division. But Rodrigues' arrival proved to be a headache to him although it was not so with Mildred, who preferred his presence in the family to his absence. A situation that would have given rise to a conflict between the father and the son became self-solving luckily. On his return, Rodrigues wanted his old security job in the distillery. Maxwell's getting his degree in education increased his job prospects. So he gave way to his father. Then the only question was if Ramsay would appoint such a man of wayward ways in his service. Roger and King complimented Maxwell for his victory and for his gesture of giving way to his father. Ramsay had a good impression regarding Rodrigues's sincerity in his job. And so he took him on in his old job.

Days passed....

Rodrigues was not a changed man. He was the same wife basher. Some months passed. Soon he started creating family unrest. Maxwell was again sorry for his mother. He thought of how he and his mother had been living a peaceful life in his father's absence. 'Those good peaceful days are gone,' Maxwell thought sadly.

Rodrigues's wife bashing was on the increase. Rodrigues didn't like Mildred to work. She did not have a tearless night. 'I suffer for you and the integrity of our family,' Mildred consoled a distraught Maxwell. But to him, no consoling was enough. When the possibility of a potential danger looms large, no amount of consoling would work because the danger is still very much there, posing perennial threat to life until done away with. And it's the odds of surely doing away with the threat alone that brings consolation to one's mind and nothing else. So his mother's attempts to console him didn't work. If anything, it only ignited his disquieting thoughts.

He couldn't stand his mother's sufferings. Maxwell's mind was boggled. He thought something should be done. Then he thought of his friend's words: 'If you get an appointment for a job, in a distant place, how can you leave your mother with your senseless drunkard father? How can you be sure he would not kill her in one of his drunken brawls with her? It's a problem which you're going to face sooner or later, when you cannot be a passive onlooker but be doing something, positive.'

'Yes, what my friend warned me some time ago seems to be prophetic. Now I'm placed in that identical situation. But what to do?' He had sleepless nights. 'How long can I pull on in this fashion? Then it's my duty to put an end to father's wayward behaviour. But how can I? If he asks me out of this house, as he had warned me once, it will be hell for me till I get a job, though my mother would come to my rescue. But what kind of rescue? She cannot come out of the house and stay with me, supporting me with her salary till I get a job, though she could. But that will never be, going by her strong yearnings for the integrity of the family. My mother wants Father and me to stay with her for the integrity of our family. She is adamant about the integrity of the family. That was why when Father was away she was sad. The depth of her desire for the integrity of our family is abysmal and unfathomable',Maxwell soliloquised.

Chapter 40

'How would it be like if I could tame your father ?' Mildred asked Maxwell once.

'So you want to invite more trouble?' Maxwell asked.

'There's already trouble. Then there's no question of my inviting trouble.' Mildred paused.

'If you make any such attempts, it will be hell for you, I swear,' Maxwell said.

'Even if that's so, there's nothing wrong in making a try. If my attempts bear fruits, isn't it a welcome proposition? And if it fails, it won't make things further worse. Do you get me, right?' Mildred asked in a logical vein.

'Yes, your logic is good. Of course, if it works. But your attempts are likely to make things worse for you,' Maxwell replied.

'What brings such negative thoughts in you?' Mildred asked.

'You can't brand it as negative thoughts. It's the most reasonable and probable consequence, if one is to draw a dispassionate conclusion from the past. We draw conclusions from our experience. And to think of something different to happen, contrary to the usual happenings, there's an appropriate word to call it . . .' Maxwell stopped halfway.

'What's that appropriate word? Why you stopped halfway?' Mildred asked.

'It's wishful thinking, simply,' Maxwell replied.

'What's it? I don't get it, all right?' Mildred said.

'It's believing something to be true because one hopes it were true,' Maxwell said.

'But I feel it would be true,' Mildred said.
'It's the same as what I said,' Maxwell said.

'It's not mine, but yours is a kind of wishful thinking. That's what I feel,' Mildred replied.

'But my thoughts are never wishful thinking. I base my view on my father's wayward behaviour, which is his second nature. Wasn't he a thoroughly unreliable man with unsteady habits? And his leaving home without a word to anyone shows he won't have any compunction to be away from home any longer. He has little concern for his family. He hadn't given a thought as to how his family lived on in his absence. Mom, I tell you, don't have high hopes about Father. Such thoughts are futile ones,' Maxwell cautioned.

Chapter 41

Then the worse happened. One day, Rodrigues came fully drunk, as usual. Mildred was not home yet. This was the first occasion that Mildred wasn't home when Rodrigues came. This situation ignited his anger.

'Where were you all these time?' Rodrigues exploded. 'I had some extra work at Petronio's,' Mildred said softly. 'And are you paid for the overtime?' Rodrigues seethed in rage.

'No,' Mildred replied.

'Then do you know you aren't supposed to work overtime for a song?' Rodrigues hissed out.

'It was on compassionate grounds. Petronio was sick and she asked my help. Is it a big crime to do a help? Moreover, I'm not that late for you to grill me in this fashion. And for that matter, who are you to question me when your own hands aren't clean? Are you a family man? Where were you during the last one year? Don't you owe me an explanation? But did you do that? All my life, I have been suffering you silently. First of all, you discipline yourself and then try to discipline me. And I tell you why was I late today. There was a meeting at the Petronio's. It was for the empowerment of women. It was a study class on how to tackle husbands like you, who make family life hell. And I have been selected as the secretary of the association for the Vypeen area. And I would like to warn you in unmistakable terms that hereafter you have to pull yourself when you are angry or I will not be the same Mildred to you. I'm enlightened. I'm empowered,' Mildred replied, which again provoked Rodrigues.

Mildred was severely bashed that day. She fell on to the ground, losing her balance, before Maxwell came running to her rescue. Mildred became unconscious. King and Roger were informed. They too dashed to Rodrigues's house. They took her to the hospital. Her condition was serious. She had a spine injury. She was put on the ventilator when she developed breathing trouble. After a week, she regained her consciousness. She was unable to move her legs. The doctor who examined her proclaimed she was paralysed below her midriff and that she would not get back to her old normal condition. The incident was a bolt from the blue to Maxwell. He spent his days nursing his mother. Mildred's condition caused her to lose her job at Petronia's house and her income stopped too. Then they all had to depend solely on the income of Rodrigues. Maxwell was in such a deplorable plight.

Chapter 42

It was in this inescapable situation that Maxwell got an appointment order from Bhave's School, Churchgate, Mumbai, posting him as a teacher in mathematics. He was to join duty within five days of receipt of the appointment order. Instead of becoming happy, Maxwell became confused and agitated.

'How can I leave my invalid mother alone with my irresponsible father to suffer his wayward, unsteady habits? Isn't it the time when she very much needs my presence?' Maxwell thought sadly.

Past thoughts came rushing to him. Maxwell remembered his mother's loving words: 'It's not long before you were off my teats'. It brought him to the knowledge how fondly his mother had nursed the thought in her motherly mind even after a long time!

Once she had declared that her suffering under her cruel husband was for the sake of her own son and the well-being of the family. There was a time when Maxwell would face rejection at the hands of his wayward father. It was his mother who gave him support. But now she was very much in need of her son's help. He remembered the assurance he had given his mother that he would not leave her alone wherever he was, which gave her confidence. Now torn between his job prospects and his mother's protection, Maxwell couldn't come to a decision. But he still continued in his reverie.

'I cannot reject the job offer at any cost. Apart from my parents, I have a life of my own. And when the opportunity for a job knocks at my door, shouldn't I seize it? One has to accept the job at any cost, in whatever inconvenient circumstances the offer comes,' he thought, firming up his mind. He decided to take up the job at any cost. At the same time, he couldn't even imagine leaving his mother in her present condition. He became quite agitated. It was a situation when Maxwell's agitation worked up sky high . . .

As a last straw, Maxwell hopefully thought his friend who had warned him of such a situation when he got a job could suggest a way out. So he decided to meet him for advice the next morning.

Chapter 43

Then something happened that night. In the morning, a shocking piece of news spread like wildfire in the locality and people poured into Maxwell's house. Those who could not get into the house stood in front of an open window, jostling and struggling on their toes and craning their necks to have a look inside. Mildred was lying on her bed as if in sleep; she was dead.

Cardiac arrest was considered to be the cause of death. The burial was slated to take place that day itself, as Maxwell had to leave for Mumbai the next day to take up the job.

That fateful night, his father had come home late. But as usual, in his inebriated condition, he started shouting at Mildred for some time. Then he left the house soon after, uttering curses. Maxwell saw him entering the house and leaving, which was most unusual. Once he reached home in the evening, Rodrigues was never in the habit of going out again. So his behaviour was strange.

The local priest was summoned to do the last rites before the burial. Maxwell's father, Rodrigues, was nowhere to be seen. The body was kept till evening, but he never turned up. So the burial took place in his absence.

Chapter 44

With the death of his mother, Maxwell felt as if his pet bird had flown away. Home was not his worry any more. A kind of mental detachment set in and he turned to himself. His own welfare became his only concern.

'Mumbai will help me forget my unhappy experiences. Now my mind is attached to Bhave's School. The past is something to be forgotten and the present is for preparing for a bright future,' Maxwell philosophized, as the train carrying him to Mumbai chugged off the Ernakulam South Railway Station. 'The idea of leaving my mother with my father had been a thorn in my flesh. Now I need not worry, though it is a sad loss for me. Keeping me busy is the only way to regain some peace of mind,' Maxwell thought.

Chapter 45

Back home, things took a different turn. Rodrigues's absence at the funeral and thereafter raised doubts in the minds of the people.

The police were alerted who as usual tried to shun their duty by writing off the death as natural. The secretary of the local Human Rights Association had filed a complaint for unnatural death, which led to an argument between him and the station house officer.

'Why are you so much interested in this matter?' asked the SHO.

'A serious human rights problem is involved in this case,' the secretary replied.

'Don't you know a dead person has no rights under the Indian law? And what human rights you're talking about? And we have many other important duties to be carried out for the people and the society,' the SHO said.

He continued, 'Do you know the Home Minister is visiting here for the inauguration of a beauty parlour with latest amenities? And I have to escort him till he leaves my jurisdiction. And do you know a minister's visit is more important to us than a dead body? Last time, the minister came here to inaugurate a slaughterhouse. And the worst had happened. Half an hour before the minister's arrival, a dead body surfaced in the river in my jurisdiction, which got hooked to the shrubs sticking out into the water from its bank. We had no time. I had to use my wits to tackle the situation. I ordered the body to be pushed off its hook, and it sailed and sailed into the jurisdiction of the neighbouring police station and then it was their worry. And in that way I saved the situation.'

'Sir, there is a serious human rights' problem involved, which you cannot ignore,' the secretary replied.

'Haven't you understood what I said? I told you in unmistakable terms not to trouble me. And mind you, if you hang around here speaking of human rights and things like that, you would be framed as the first accused in this murder,' the SHO shouted angrily.

'But, sir, you know . . .'

Before the secretary could complete his sentence, the SHO jumped to his feet. 'You bastard! Don't you understand what I said? You stupid ass! Get lost! Will you?' the SHO blared.

However, the people of the locality did not give up, and the police could no longer ignore the public uprising. Soon the dead body was exhumed for post-mortem. The doctor noticed a needle mark at the back of the corpse. Chemical examination found the cause of the death was murder by injecting poison. All fingers pointed to Rodrigues, who had been absconding since the death took place. A case was registered and Rodrigues was nabbed.

Chapter 46

Maxwell was summoned to appear before the court as a witness. During the examination, Maxwell did not give any evidence to protect his father. He seemed very agitated. He showed an indifference towards his father.

Maxwell was put in the witness box.

You're Maxwell Rodrigues?", the prosecutor asked

"Yes, I am", Maxwell replied.

"That night, when did you go to sleep?",the prosecutor inquired

"At 10 p.m", Maxwell replied.

"On that day, when did the accused come home?",the prosecutor asked

"It was past midnight", Maxwell answered.

"Could you cite the exact time?", the prosecutor asked "I can't", Maxwell replied.

"Were you awake when the accused came in?", the prosecutor asked

"Yes, I saw my father walking in, with unsure steps. Then I heard him shouting at my mother for some time ", Maxwell replied.

"And then?", the prosecutor asked

"After half an hour, he left hastily, in a huff, uttering some curses", Maxwell replied

"Was your father in the habit of leaving home after coming home in the night?", the prosecutor asked

"No. This was the first occasion, as far as I know", Maxwell answered.

"Are you sure the person who came in was your father?", the prosecutor inquired.

"Yes", Maxwell replied.

"How did you know?",the prosecutor asked

"I saw him and I can distinguish his voice too", Maxwell replied.

"Aren't you in the habit of locking all the doors at night?", the prosecutor asked

"All but one, as I am not sure when my father would be home", Maxwell replied.

"That's all, Your Honour", the prosecutor, turning to the judge.

Then ten more were examined as prosecution witnesses, whose depositions all corroborated Maxwell's . . .

Rodrigues was questioned by the court, on the basis of evidence, who denied the charge. But he submitted to the court he had no evidence to adduce.

The case was adjourned for arguments. Meanwhile, the prosecutor sought the court's permission for Maxwell to leave for Mumbai, to join duty as his presence was no longer needed, which was allowed by the court.

Chapter 47

As the train carrying Maxwell back to Mumbai, moved off the Ernakulam Railway Station, gory, unpleasant thoughts started troubling him. 'How my mother suffered at the hands of my father. How he used to bully her! Their life had always been one of confrontation,' Maxwell thought sadly.

Throughout the journey, he was haunted by the thoughts of God, death, murder, sufferings,Euthanasia etc.

Thinking of God, he thought, 'Is man the creation of God or God the creation of man?' Thinking of death, he thought, 'Sure, death is a cure, a panacea for all human ills, worries, miseries, and hardships in life. Endless torture is crueller than death itself.' Maxwell then thought of euthanasia, the modern concept that caters to end the lives of those who are destined to suffer from incurable disease. But then he thought that the law of the land wouldn't allow the legalisation of it.

Reaching the Victoria terminus, the train soon came to a grinding halt. Maxwell reached the school and joined duty immediately, thinking that work was the best way to take the load off his mind. But he was glued to the thought that he ought to have done something to save his mother's life; after all, it was his pious obligation.

Within a week, the arguments of the case were over and Rodrigues was pronounced guilty, going by the strong circumstantial evidence presented by the prosecution. He was given life imprisonment and he did not prefer to appeal.

That day, a kind of gloom engulfed Maxwell; his mind was heavy and restless. After the verdict was given, Maxwell didn't bother about the welfare of his father, who spent his days behind the bars. Rodrigues was calm, accepting it as his fate, but Maxwell's mind was in conflict. The nagging thought that as a son he had failed miserably in saving his mother's life followed him like a shadow wherever he went.

Soon Maxwell began to feel that he should get out of Mumbai too. He was afraid of meeting people from his native place, who frequented Mumbai more than any other place in India. And meeting them disturbed his peace of mind.

Then he remembered an advertisement in the newspaper, inviting applications for teacher's post in mathematics in a school in Nagaland. He pulled out that day's newspaper which had been discarded after reading, as he was already employed and no longer needed a job. Luckily, the date of the interview was not over. A sigh of relief escaped him. So before making sure about the job in Nagaland, he resigned from Bhave's School and left for Nagaland.

Chapter 48

Soon Maxwell found himself employed in St Benedict School in Kohima, the capital of Nagaland.

Maxwell liked the place very much. The cool climate, the beautiful terrain of mountains, the lush green valleys, the rivers, ponds, flowers all held a special charm for him. Barring the occasional terrorist activities, the people were generally calm and gentle and the atmosphere was friendly. This ambience could do something to make his agitated mind relaxed.

Then with the change of seasons, there was an epidemic of chicken pox in Kohima, which caused a fall in the attendance of the students. Soon after the students started coming back to school, Maxwell noticed some boils on his body. He had a severe infection of chicken pox and was admitted to Kohima's hospital for infectious diseases.

The nurse who attended to him was Nagma, a Naga girl who did not have typical Naga features. Every morning, noon, evening, and night, she visited Maxwell's room to administer medicines. Every morning, she came smartly dressed in the nurse's white uniform and greeted him pleasantly. As she would walk away, Maxwell would keep watching her till she disappeared into the next room.

Once as he was watching her leaving the room, she suddenly looked back and gave a smile. Maxwell smiled back, his joy knowing no bounds.

Another day, as he was lost in his thoughts about her beauty, someone tapped his shoulder gently. He woke up from his thoughts with a start and found it was none other than Nagma. Suddenly he blushed.

'What were you thinking of, looking through the window?' she asked casually.

Unaware that she had entered the room, her sudden question embarrassed him. He hemmed and hawed and groped for words for a moment. Then he salvaged the situation by asking a counter question,

'Where do you stay?'

'In a convent.'

'Your parents, sisters, and brothers?' Maxwell inquired.

'I have none. I'm an orphan. I was brought up in the convent, where I stay now,' Nagma said.

The reply made Maxwell happy. As Nagma was about to leave the room, he asked, 'How long have I to stay in bed?' 'Be patient till you cease to be a patient. And why are you in a hurry to leave? Don't you like being here?' Nagma

asked with a smile.

Maxwell liked the pun upon the word 'patient' and smiled back at her.

Now Maxwell's mind was always full of Nagma and he was curious to know what she thought of him. One evening, Nagma made an unscheduled visit to Maxwell's room. She was off duty and had come just to chat with him. She told him, trying to sound casual, that the nuns of the convent were trying to find a bridegroom for her. Mustering all his courage, he promptly asked, 'May I ask you one personal question?'

'Please feel free,' Nagma said politely, looking at him encouragingly.

'Are you attached to anyone?' Maxwell queried politely.

'I'm not. The Nagas are very race conscious. They have very high clannish spirits. They won't allow a Naga boy or a girl to marry outside their tribe. There are as many as sixteen tribes here.

'An adventurous outsider who ventures to marry a Naga girl has either to elope with her from Nagaland or face death. It's the custom of the elders to kill such erratic youths and proudly display their scalps strung around their neck.

'However, they have no objection to a half Naga marrying an outsider. In my case, I'm not a pure Naga, so I can't get attached to a Naga boy.'

Taking his cue from her account, Maxwell gained courage. 'Then how come are you a half Naga?' he asked.

'My mother was pure Naga. She belonged to the Angami tribe. But my father was a soldier from Punjab. He cheated her. All his promises to marry my mother and take her away to Punjab were broken when he learnt that she was pregnant.

'One day he decamped without a word to her and she took refuge in the convent. The kind nuns there kept her in the convent in hiding till I was born. Then she left me with the nuns and went in search of her lover. And she never came back,' Nagma concluded, her eyes brimming with tears.

Maxwell then proposed to her. And she readily agreed to marry him. But they had to wait till he was back on his feet, and with the blessings of the nuns, they were married within a month.

Chapter 49

As the days passed, Nagma showed her inquisitiveness about Maxwell's past, his family, and how he happened to come to Nagaland.

Hesitating at first because it would rekindle the gory past in his mind, he reluctantly agreed to reveal the details about him.

'I hail from Vypeen island, Kochi. My father, Rodrigues Noronah, was a drunkard. He was very cruel and he used to beat my mother regularly, coming home every night fully drunk.' Maxwell tried to be brief, but the information ignited Nagma's inquisitiveness all the more.

'Then how did you dare to leave your mother with such a cruel man and come to work in a distant place like Nagaland?' Nagma asked in surprise.

'My mother was killed the day before I was to leave for Mumbai to join Bhave's School,' replied Maxwell.

'Murdered!' she asked, rather shocked. 'Yes,' replied Maxwell, sounding jittery.

'Who committed the cruel act?' Nagma persisted. 'I'm not sure.' Maxwell sounded confused.

'Wasn't there a police case?' Nagma asked, exasperated when Maxwell nodded his head in affirmation.

Nagma continued, 'And what was the outcome of the case?'

'My father was found guilty,' Maxwell replied.

For some time, Nagma was thoughtful. But she was not satisfied.

'Were you home when the murder took place?' she asked anxiously.

'I was home that night,' Maxwell replied.

'Then kindly describe the situation in which your mother was killed.' Nagma was in extreme anguish.

'In the dead of night, my father came home. I saw him wading in. After some time, I heard him shout at my mother and then he went out of the house hastily, in a huff, shouting some curses. The next morning, she was found dead. The court found strong links of circumstantial evidence and sentenced him to life imprisonment . . .' Maxwell trailed off.

This explanation did not go down well with Nagma. She found an inconsistency.

'Did you hear your mother say anything to your father, when he was shouting at her, or did you hear your mother giving out at least a cry for help . . . ? Had your father killed your mother, you would surely have heard her cry in alarm or some noise in her extreme anguish, as you say you were awake at that time. I'm sure that your mother died long before your father's arrival . . . That he is not the murderer . . .

'When your father was shouting at your mother, there was no reply from her, going by your version. What does this show? That your father had been shouting at a lifeless corpse,' Nagma declared emphatically.

'Now who else could be the culprit? And what was his intention?' Nagma asked with the expertise of a criminal lawyer.

Maxwell, though silent, was wonderstruck at her incisive clarity and unbroken continuity of thoughts in shaping the line of her reasoning.

'I think you could surely give me a clue about the real culprit,' Nagma persisted.

Maxwell was in extreme distress. Past thoughts came rushing to his mind. He began to shiver; his lips moved to say something, but no words issued forth.

'You seem to be morbidly afraid of revealing the name of the culprit,' Nagma asserted. 'Come on, tell me did anybody threaten you not to disclose his name?' Nagma asked emphatically.

Nagma's incessant questioning pierced through him like a knife through butter. He was losing his power of resistance. At the same time, he looked morbidly afraid to reveal the name of the culprit. The more she insisted, the more he stared at her dumbfounded. Nagma was sure Maxwell knew the culprit and that the guy had threatened him not to disclose his name. So Nagma decided she would give him all assurance and bring out the name of the culprit at any cost. Maxwell was under heavy pressure. And the pressure from Nagma was mounting. Maxwell could not keep the name of the culprit a secret any more. And he swooned. When he regained his consciousness, he was lying with his head in the lap of his dear wife, who was gently messaging his shoulders.

'Calm down, Maxwell,' Nagma told him with concern. 'Don't be afraid of telling me the truth. Who performed the cruel act? What was his intention?'

Maxwell looked helplessly into her beautiful eyes with those fluttering eyelids. In his emotional stress, they held no charm for him.

Suddenly, to the utter dismay of Nagma, cursing himself and those ephemeral moments which he fervently wished had never existed in his life at all, during which he lost all his senses, during which his thoughts ran amok, and during which he acted in a fit of frenzy, he whimpered, 'It . . . was . . . a . . . mercy . . . killing . . .' And he began to sob like a baby.

Muvattupuzha,
1-3-2015